Lavinia Stowell.

Des Moines.

Iowa.

LUCILE.

Journal

Amy Zoe Mason

Found by
Kristine Atkinson and Joyce Atkinson

Simon & Schuster
New York • London • Toronto • Sydney

F
ATK
c. 1

SIMON & SCHUSTER
Rockefeller Center
1230 Avenue of the Americas
New York, NY 10020

SIMON & SCHUSTER and colophon are registered trademarks of Simon & Schuster, Inc.
For information regarding special discounts for bulk purchases, please contact Simon & Schuster Special Sales at 1-800-456-6798 or business@simonandschuster.com

Manufactured in the UK by Butler and Tanner

10 9 8 7 6 5 4 3 2 1

ISBN-13: 978-0-7432-9038-8
ISBN-10:   0-7432-9038-0

A few months ago we bought a small desk at the Blue Bird Circle Resale Shop in Houston. It was a pretty little desk, but it needed to be refinished. When we refinished it, we took out the drawers and we were surprised to find a secret compartment behind one of the drawers. This journal was hidden in that compartment.

Kristine Atkinson
Joyce Atkinson

those who wish to sing, always find a song.

Post Card

U.S. POSTAGE
2 CENTS 2

Amy Zoe Mason
2609 Violet Lane
Houston, Texas 77019

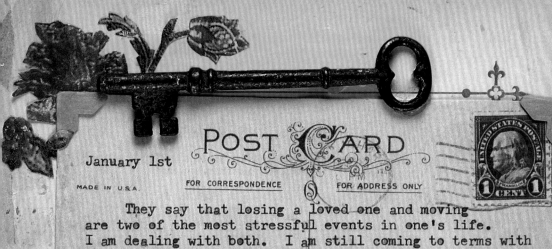

They say that losing a loved one and moving
are two of the most stressful events in one's life.
I am dealing with both. I am still coming to terms with
my mother's sudden death just two months ago. And we
will be moving from Houston to Massachusetts this spring.
I know that dealing with these two changes, as well as
taking care of our children will be more difficult
because I will be doing it on my own. Bob has to leave
in three days to start work in Boston.

   I hope that keeping a journal/scrapbook will help
me with my feelings of loss and help me face the changes
ahead.

I have tried to keep a journal before,
but writing isn't easy for me. I express
my self better with images. That's why I
have always loved creating scrapbooks for our
family memories.

   I recently saw some beautiful Altered Books and the
idea really appealed to me. In an altered book I can
express myself in writing and collages. Doing this on
an old printed page seems less intimidating than a blank
page in a new journal.

   I bought this book several years ago because I liked
the cover. It cost 25 cents. A lot of the pages were
water damaged or torn, so I don't feel that I am damaging
a book, rather I am giving it a new life.

Out of suffering comes creativity.

The artist is a receptacle for emotions that come from all over the place: from the sky, from the earth, from a scrap of paper, from a passing shape, from a spider's web.

Mary Susan Adams

Mother Friend
Gardener Musician
Grandmother

Dear Mom,
I miss you everyday.
I feel your presence everywhere--
but especially in our garden. You and I were always so
close, maybe because it was just the two of us for so
long. Bob always said that he couldn't imagine a better
mother-in-law. He loved it as much as I did when you
moved in with us. And our children had the most loving
grandmother in the world. I can't believe
that you are gone.

Green fingers are the extension of a verdant heart.

You will always live in my heart

There is a time for some things, and a time for all things; a time for great things, and a time for small things

Exciting times for the Mason Family!

We will be moving from Houston to Boston because of Daddy's new job.

THE WENTWORTH HEART I
ROBERT M. MASON, M.D.,
DIRECTOR

PHOTO: E. RUSSELL

Wentworth Heart Institute Appoints Director

Robert M. Mason, M.D. has been appointed Director of the new Wentworth Heart Institute. Funded by the Jonathan and Julia Wentworth Foundation, The Wentworth Heart Institute will be a world leader in cardiac care and research. Dr. Mason come to The Wentworth Heart Institute from the prestigious Texas Medical Center in Houston.

"Choosing Dr. Mason was one of my best decisions," said Julia Wentworth. "His cutting edge research in cardiac care and

Aunt Flo's Cherry Nut Cake

2 cups sugar
2 cups flour
2 teaspoons soda
1/2 teaspoon salt

2 eggs, beaten
2 Tablespoons melted butter
1 can pitted red cherries drained
1 1/2-2 cups chopped nuts

Sift together sugar, flour, soda, salt
Combine eggs, butter and add to dry ingredients with cherries. Stir in nuts.
Pour into greased and floured 9x13 pan.
Bake @ 350°. Serve warm with Hot Butter Sauce

Hot Butter Sauce

1 cup sugar
1/2 cup butter
1 cup cream
2 teaspoons vanilla

} Stir together all ingredients and cook over low heat, stirring frequently, about 15 minutes or until saucy not thick. Pour over cake.

This cake is an old family recipe from Mom's Great Aunt Flo.

We made Daddy's favorite dinner

'If he love her,' he thought, ...
Then he turn'd to the future—and order'd his dinner.

Menu

Bruchetta
Grilled Salmon with Holidays Sauce
Cesar Salad
Grilled Asperagus
Aunt Flo's Cherry Nut Cake

XIX.

We may live without poetry, music, and art;
We may live without conscience, and live without heart;
We may live without friends; we may live without
  books;
But civilized man cannot live without cooks.
He may live without books,—what is knowledge but
  grieving?
He may live without hope,—what is hope but deceiv-
  ing?
He may live without love,—what is passion but pin-
  ing?
But where is the man that can live without dining?

Darling,
I am going
to miss you.
I love you.
Bob

Franc jeu! on the
Ask!

Duke, you
You remember it you with
When you went: and
We met, you greeted me, then with a brow
Bright with triumph: your words (you remember
them now?
Were: Let us be friends?

LUVOIS.

Well!

ALFRED.

How then, after that,
Can you and she meet as acquaintances?

LUVOIS.

Did she not then, herself, the Comtesse de Nevers
Solve your riddle to-night with those soft lips of hers?

ALFRED.

In our converse to-night we avoided the past;
But the question I ask should be answered at last
By you, if you will; if you will not, by her.

LUVOIS.

Indeed? but that question, milord, can it stir
Such an interest in you if your passion be dead?

ALFRED.

Yes. Esteem may remain, although love be no more.
Lucile asked me, this night, to my wife (understand
To my wife!) to present her. I did so. Her hand

There is only one happiness in life, to love and be loved.
George Sand

Darling,

I'm at the Ritz-Carlton. You would love it. My suite is big enough for our whole family.

These next few months will be hard, but I'm sure that I was right about not uprooting Alex and Susan so soon after your mother's death. I can spend time getting to know the area better, so we can find just the right house for us. And I'll be able to come home most weekends.

Hope you find a good real estate agent. You should probably talk to the agent that Dr. Martin recommended, Vanessa Garamond. He said that she was very good. But make sure you choose the one that you feel most comfortable with, since you are the one that will be working with her. I'm sorry that I'm not there to help you.

I'll talk to you tomorrow.
Kiss the kids for me.
I wish you were here in my arms.

Bob

Cleaning out Mom's apartment over our garage has been so hard--so many memories. It makes me feel closer to Mom, but it makes me miss her even more. I found these old recipes. I also found Dad's old manual typewriter.

Jeanette's Orange Rolls

- 1/2 c. milk, warmed
- 1/4 c. sugar
- 1/2 tsp. salt
- 1/4 c. shortening
- 1/4 c. Orange Juice
- 1 Tblsp. orange rind
- 1 pkg. yeast
- 1 egg, beaten
- 2 1/2 c. flour

Knead well.
Let rise until double
Punch down
Shape in rolls and let rise until double.
Bake at 400° 12 min

Pour over hot rolls:

- 1/2 c. powdered sugar
- 1 T. orange juice
- 1/2 T. orange rind

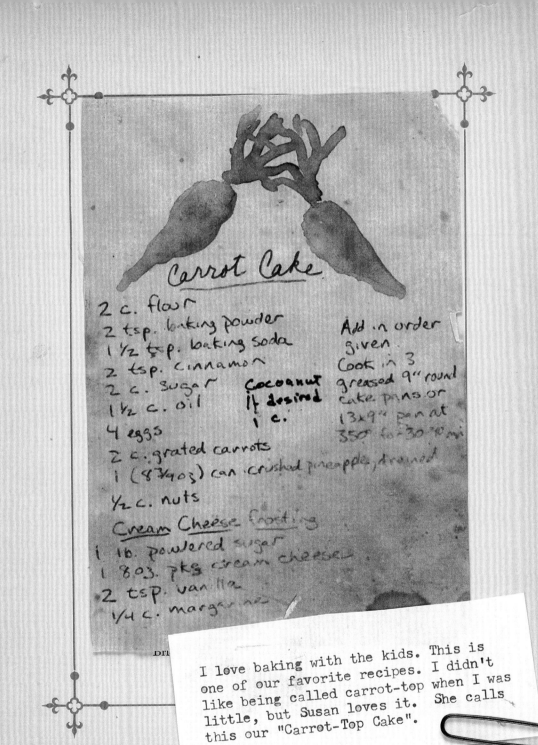

Carrot Cake

2 c. flour
2 tsp. baking powder
1 ½ tsp. baking soda
2 tsp. cinnamon
2 c. sugar   Cocoanut
1 ½ c. oil   If desired
                          1 c.
4 eggs
2 c. grated carrots
1 (8¾ oz) can crushed pineapple, drained

½ c. nuts

Add in order
given.
Cook in 3
greased 9" round
cake pans or
13x9" pan at
350° for 30-40 min

Cream Cheese Frosting
1 lb. powdered sugar
1 8 oz. pkg cream cheese
2 tsp. vanilla
¼ c. margarine

I love baking with the kids. This is
one of our favorite recipes. I didn't
like being called carrot-top when I was
little, but Susan loves it. She calls
this our "Carrot-Top Cake".

POST CARD

Dear Susan and Alex,
I miss you already.
I hope that you had
fun at The Dessert
Gallery on The way
home. I would love
a piece of their
cheesecake right now.
It would be better than
airplane food.
Kiss Mommy for me.
Talk to you tonight
Love, Daddy

Old North Church, Boston, Massachusetts

The Masons
2609 Violet Lane
Houston Tx. 77019

I LIKE AIRPLANES

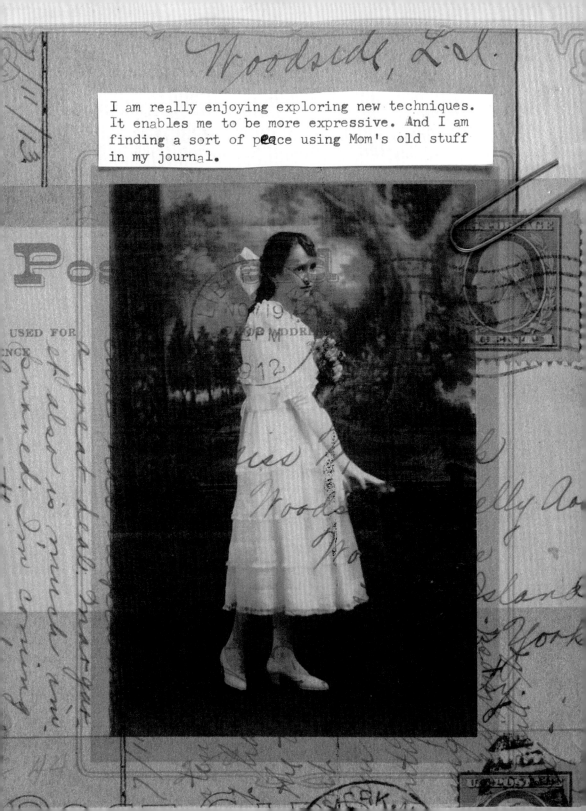

I am really enjoying exploring new techniques. It enables me to be more expressive. And I am finding a sort of peace using Mom's old stuff in my journal.

The After Christmas Tree Party was
bittersweet--the children all really
enjoyed it, but it was Mom's tradition.
I hope that it helps to keep Mom's
memory alive for Susan and Alex.

Saturday we had to go to the Arts
Festival. It made me feel out of
place to go to a family event without
Bob.

Here's an after
Christmas ornament
from Boston. It
can be the first
one on our
first Boston tree
Love,
Daddy

It was so thoughtful of Bob to send
us the ornament.

Please come to our
After Christmas Tree Party.
We have moved our tree to the
backyard. Please help us decorate it
with food for the birds for the winter.

Sunday, 2-4pm
Susan Mason
Alex Mason
2609 Violet Lane

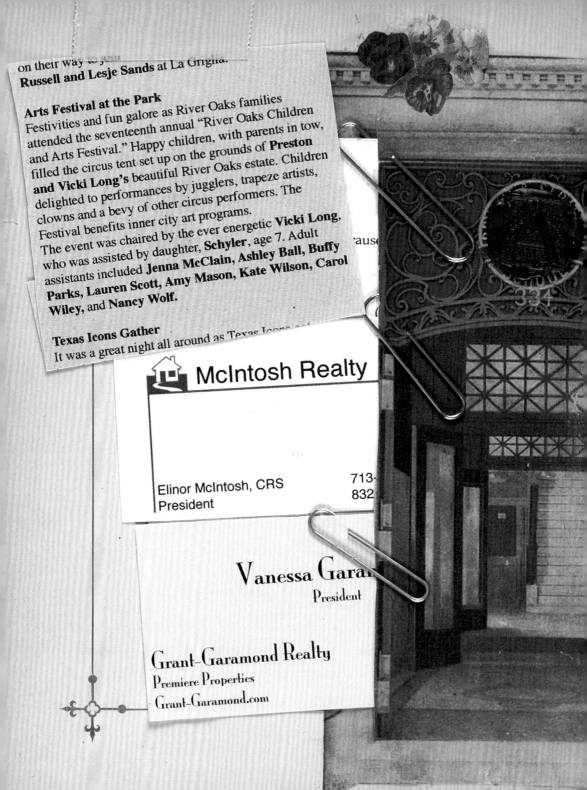

on their way to join
Russell and Lesje Sands at La Griglia.

Arts Festival at the Park
Festivities and fun galore as River Oaks families attended the seventeenth annual "River Oaks Children and Arts Festival." Happy children, with parents in tow, filled the circus tent set up on the grounds of **Preston and Vicki Long's** beautiful River Oaks estate. Children delighted to performances by jugglers, trapeze artists, clowns and a bevy of other circus performers. The Festival benefits inner city art programs.
The event was chaired by the ever energetic **Vicki Long**, who was assisted by daughter, **Schyler**, age 7. Adult assistants included **Jenna McClain, Ashley Ball, Buffy Parks, Lauren Scott, Amy Mason, Kate Wilson, Carol Wiley,** and **Nancy Wolf.**

Texas Icons Gather
It was a great night all around as Texas Icons

McIntosh Realty

Elinor McIntosh, CRS
President

713-
832-

Vanessa Garai
President

Grant-Garamond Realty
Premiere Properties
Grant-Garamond.com

--- Amy Mason <amyzmason@yahoo.com> wrote:
> Hi Bob,
>   I interviewed the 3 real estate agents. They all
> seemed good. Mrs. McIntosh was really nice and very
> experienced, but she sort of reminded me of Mom, and
> it made me sad. I think that I will choose Vanessa
> Garamond. I looked her up on the internet (articles
> attached) She is so successful and very friendly. I
> know that she will do a good job.
>   Got to go pick up Susan and Alex at school, and
> then piano lessons.
>   Love Amy
>

Hi Ames,
Vanessa Garamond sounds like a good choice, but it's
up to you. From those articles you found on the
internet, she sounds very successful. I'm sure that
she'll be great.
    That's funny that she lives in the Huntington, and
pointed out her exact apartment when she was on our
patio. Talk about local. When we look up and see the
Huntington, I never thought about someone looking down
at us, but I'm sure from up there they can't see the
houses through all the trees. River Oaks must look
like a forest.
    Tell Susan I'm proud that she got a star from the
dentist. And Alex better work harder on brushing his
teeth.
    Kiss the kids for me.
    I wish that you were in my arms.
    Love Bob

Grant-Garamond

Vanessa Garamon

Grant-Garamond
Premiere Real Es

Garamond Awarded Golden Key for Top Sales in River Oaks Area

Vanessa Garamond, President/Owner of Grant-Garamond Realty, has been awarded the River Oaks Golden Key by the River Oaks Area Realtors Association (ROARA). The Golden Key is the top honor awarded to Real Estate Professionals in the River Oaks Area. Vanessa Garamond has been President of Grant-Garamond Realty for the last two years, assuming the presidency/ownership upon the death of company founder William Kent Grant. Grant-Garamond Realty has been a leader in premiere residential sales for more than 40 years.

Bayou Bend Gala Planned

Bayou Bend Friends have announced the date of the 25th annual spring gala. "Azaleas in Bloom" will be held on the evening of March 1, at Bayou Bend Gardens. Vanessa Garamond, Chair of this year's gala said, "We have exciting plans for this year. It will be the best celebration ever. We expect to raise more money for local charities this year than ever before."

Garamond to be President

Grant-Garamond Realty announced today that Vanessa Garamond will assume the position of President, following the unexpected death of William Grant last month. Ms. Garamond has been associated with the company for over fifteen years. She became a licensed real estate agent shortly before she joined Grant Realty. Garamond quickly became the top producer in the company and in the River Oaks area. Founder William Kent Grant conferred full partner status on Garamond four years ago, changing the firm's name to Grant-Garamond Realty. Grant left sole proprietorship of the firm to Garamond. Garamond is as well known for her fundraising as for her business success. She has chaired a wide variety of charity events including "Azaleas in Bloom" at Bayou Bend, numerous galas for both the Art Museum and the Opera and the much anticipated annual "Mardi Gras Madness" which benefits the Medical Center.

Vanessa Garamond
President

Grant-Garamond Realty
Premiere Properties
Grant-Garamond.com

Business Leader Found Dead in Home

HOUSTON — Prominent Houston businessman and philanthropist, William Kent Grant, 68, was found dead in his River Oaks home Friday of an apparent sleeping pill overdose. Grant was founder and co-owner of Grant-Garamond Realty. Grant had been active in Houston real estate for over 40 years.

Grant originally moved to Houston in 1961 and soon opened Grant Realty, concentrating on River Oaks properties. For the last eight years, Grant-Garamond has been the leading producer in the River Oaks area, specializing in estate properties.

Grant was married to Houston debutante Elizabeth Brown in 1963. The couple was prominent in Houston society. Mrs. Grant died four years ago, after a long battle with cancer. The Grants had no children.

According to Ilse Hemmings, Mr. Grant's longtime secretary, he had been devastated by his wife's death, but in the last two years had developed a strong interest in sculpting and seemed much happier. Hemmings said that Grant had plans to sell his share of the agency and move to Florence, Italy to pursue his art studies.

"I know that Mr. Grant sometimes had trouble sleeping, but he was excited about his plans to move to Italy. I know his overdose had to be an accident," said Vanessa Garamond, Grant's business partner. "Houston has lost a great man. Our agency will continue his legacy of excellence."

Grant-Garamond Realty

Dear Amy —

I enjoyed meeting you to discuss listing your home. You have created a home with warmth and charm.

I hope that you have had time to look through the information that I left for you.

I look forward to meeting with you on Thursday to discuss my marketing plans for your home.

Thank you,

Vanessa

To: amyzmason@yahoo.com

Darling,

I'm here in my temporary office.

I met with Mrs. Wentworth for breakfast, and then we came here to The Institute. The construction is progressing nicely. Mrs. Wentworth knows just what she wants. She is committed to creating a world-class cardiology center. I am so fortunate to be part of it. It is exciting and challenging to be involved from this early stage. Mrs. Wentworth thinks that the biggest challenge for you will be meeting the social expectations that will come to you as the wife of the director. I am sure that you will rise to the occasion.

Kiss the kids for me,
I wish you were here in my arms.
Bob

Taking a chance at something new in
the near future will pay off.

it ... ... see through the ...
exist, the surrounding graves, then the outNie
... and beyond to the rolling hills miles and ...

What—What ... happening to me? ...

You are coming ... age, the fox had ... with a ...
could smile, Minako could not imagine. You now ...
perceived it is not the end but the beginning, a mere isth ...
open to your budding perceptions.

How far will ... be able to see? Minako asked, ... into the dist ...

Today I walked over to River Oaks Bookstore and looked through some design books while I thought about our new house. One thing I want is a big farmhouse kitchen with a fireplace. I can see the children sitting at a beautiful old table doing homework or projects while Bob and I cook. It will be fun to go antiquing for the perfect table.

While I was browsing I ran into Meredith and her sister. We ended up having lunch at La Madeliene. I love their tomato basil soup. I wish that I had the recipe so I could make it when we move.

Through them all, past the bridge, to the wild seaside.
And there, whether he leave, or keep his wife still,
There's the free sea round him.

J. HEMINGSON
OCTO' 31 84

And all things, there, live and rejoice together,
From the frail peach-blossom that first appears

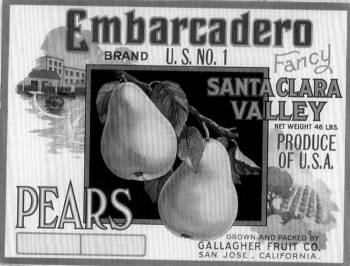

—A broken heart and a rose-roofed bower.
O oft, and in many a desolate hour,
The cold strange faces she sees shall remind her

Apple-Cranberry Cake

2 eggs
2 cups sugar
2 cups flour
2 t. cinnamon
1 t. soda

1/2 t. salt
1 t. vanilla
4 cups grated apples
1/2 cup dried cranberries
1/2 cup chopped pecans

'Shall I hear through your umbrage ancestral the wind
'Prophesy as of yore, when it shook the deep mind
'Of my boyhood, with whispers from the far years
'Of love, fame, the raptures life cooled them with tears!
'Henceforth shall the tread of a ... alone
'Rouse your echoes?'
           'O think not,' ... of the son
'Of the man whom unjustly you ... think
'Of this young ... creature, that cries from the brink
'Of a grave ... mercy!
                        ... own word
'(Words my memory mournfully ever records!)
'How with love ... the wreck ... a whole life ... torn,
   Eugene,
'Look with ... those words in ... tears!) once
   ...
... young soldier sinking ... from ...
... g'd down
By the weight of the love in his heart: ...
'No fame comforts him nations should ...
'The lone grave down to which he is ...
'Which life has rejected! Will ...
'You, with such a love's memory ... deep ... scene!
'You though ... o, while life hath ... lent to ...
'Through the ... hath wrought ... the fame ...
... hath won,
'By recalling the visions and dream ... youth; ...
'Such as lies at your door now: when ... out in ...
'To stretch forth a hand, to speak ... one word
'And by that word you rescue a life ...

Bob loves having this cake in the morning with coffee. The house smells wonderful while it is baking! And it is fat free!

Still he sought to put from him the cup; turn'd his
face
On his hands, and anon, as though wishing to chase
With one angry effort those thoughts aside
He sprang up . . . . and bitterly cried
'No!—Const . . . .
. . . . The lowest
light sudden . . . . warb'd by . . . . .
. . . . which . . . . . . eyes pour'd the light
Of their de . . . . upon him.
No wonder
He felt, as in . . . . his nature shrink under
. . . . impuls . . . . . . at grave regard . . For between
. . . . Luvois . . . the Sœur Seraphine
. . . . the height of one soul
. . . . she look'd down on him from the whole
. . . . a hei . . . There were sad nights and
. . . . long months and years in that heart-
. . . . ing gaze;
. . . . oice, when she spoke, with sharp pathos
. . . . through . . .
. . . . . . ansfix'd him.
'Eugene de Luvois, but for you,
'I might have been now—not this wandering nun,
'But a mother, a wife—pleading, not for the son
'Of another, but blessing some child of my own,
'Hi . . . the man's that I once loved . . . Hush! that

In a large mixing bowl, beat the eggs.
Add all the dry ingredients and mix together.
Stir in the apples (apples do not have to be peeled
before grating), cranberries and nuts.
    Pour into a 9x13 inch pan that has been sprayed
with Pam. Sprinkle with cinnamon sugar. Bake at
350 degrees for about 45 minutes, or until a toothpick
inserted near the center comes out clean.

Hi,

I booked a flight to arrive Friday at 7:45 pm, on Continental, flight 1283.

Sometimes I still find it hard to believe that I am the Director of the Institute. It is what I have dreamed of, and Mrs. Wentworth has made it all possible for me. Her commitment to the success of the Institute is incredible.

Can't wait to see you and kiss you and the kids myself.
Love,
Bob

your bosom, like my love there,
Just half secret and half seen;
And the soft light from above there,
Streaming o'er you where you lean,

POST CARD

GREETINGS FROM Far Far Away

23

Far Alex & Susan,
Here I am in Boston. I am at the hotel right now, but on Thursday I will be moving into Mrs. Wentworth's guesthouse. Remember you saw it in October when you were here. Susan said that it looked like a fairy tale cottage. It is nice but it will be very lonely for me. I can't wait to see you when I come home for the weekend. Kiss Mommy for me

Love Daddy

The Masons
2609 Violet Lane
Houston Tx 77019

Boston: John Hancock Building. I.M. Pei, Architect

Check...

ull to the
' In th
th the
est of
—to wa

have con

River Oaks Floral Design

Amy—
Thank you so much for entrusting me with the sale of your home. I will stop by on Saturday at 5:00 pm with some papers for you and your husband to sign.

Vanessa

- Picnic at the Beach
- Building sandcastles
- Splashing in the water
- Susan trying Bob's new digital camera
- Perfect day!

B₃ E₁ A₁ C₃ H₄

That seem'd almost stern, so intense was its still
Lofty stillness, like sunlight

When seem'd to lock up in a co

Tears harden to crystal. Yet harsh if he were,

From: "Bob Mason" <mason2609@yahoo.com>

Subject: Great Weekend

To: amyzmason@yahoo.com

Hi Honey,

What a morning, so much to do, but I'll take a minute to answer your email...Yes, it was a great weekend. What a good idea to get up early and go to the beach, the kids loved it. In this freezing weather, it's hard to believe that we were building sand castles on the beach two days ago. Susan sure loved using the digital camera. She has your artistic eye, she took some nice pictures. I think that I might pick up an inexpensive digital camera for her. I would love the kids to send me some of the pictures that they take.

Dinner Saturday night was great. I'm glad that Vanessa ended up staying for dinner. I enjoyed getting to know her. She's a live wire. It was interesting to hear about all her fundraising activities. We could use someone like her at the Institute. And she sure tells some good stories and was very funny about her love life. When she said that she has to stop choosing men based on their looks, I said, "Why, it worked for me. I only picked Amy because of her beautiful auburn hair" lol

Off to more meetings. Kiss the kids for me.
Wish you were here in my arms.
Bob

In a few days
To the angry surprise of half

Bob's Flank Steak

1 Flank Steak
1 Tablespoon Soy Sauce
1 teaspoon thyme.

Sprinkle the steak on both sides with soy sauce and thyme. Let the steak marinate for 20-30 minutes.

Grill the steak to medium rare. Slice against the grain. Serve with sauce.

Red Wine-Scallion Sauce

1 stick butter
1 cup sliced scallions (green onions)
1 cup red wine

In a sauce pan, melt the butter. Saute the scallions until tender. Add the wine. Bring to low boil for about 2 minutes.

I am starting to feel more relaxed about the move now that I have chosen a real estate agent. And Mrs. Wentworth told Bob that the kids and I should take as much time as we need to move. She seems very thoughtful.

This is my typewriter. It belonged to
my grandfather. My father⬛⬛⬛ always used
it to do his writing. One of my earliest
memories is of sitting on my father's lap
typing.

'You see that your latest command has secured
'My immediate obedience—presuming I may

nt pity, above
'The vulgar results of all pure human love :
'For we deem, with that vanity common to youth,

There is something about using the manual
typewriter that makes me feel more connected
to my writing. The typewriter becomes an extension
of my thoughts and emotions. And sometimes I find
myself really banging ⬛⬛at the keys. I love the
irregularities of the letters and even my typing
mistakes are part of the process. When I look back
at what I have written, those are the very things
that ⬛⬛⬛ help me remember how I was feeling.

I really enjoy working on my journal
in this old book. I feel more creative and I
love experimenting with new techniques. This
is the first time that I have ever liked
keeping a journal. I can certainly understand
the appeal of altered books. I feel free to try
anything.

With Bob gone I have troublesleeping so I;m
glad I have my journal and collages to work on
at night. But some times I losetrack of time and
stay up all night. I know I need more sleep.

CANTO V.]

LUCILE.

And none so beguiled and defrauded by chance,
But what once, in his life, some minute circumst...
Would have fully sufficed to secure him the blis...
Which, missing it then, he for ever must miss.
And to most of us, ere we go down to the grav...
Life, relenting, accords the good gift we woul...
But, as though by some strange imperfection...
The good gift, when it comes, comes a mo...
  late.
The Future's great veil our breath fitfully...
And behind it broods ever the mighty Pe...
Yet! there's many a slip 'twixt the cup...

From: "Bob Mason" <mason2609@yahoo.c...

Subject: Hello

To: amyzmason@yahoo.com

Hi Honey,
  That's nice for you that Vanessa is stopping by to
visit during her evening run. I can believe what
Vanessa told you about making a step-by-step plan and
always sticking to it to reach her goals. That's why
she is successful. She's very driven.
  That approach would help you grow into the
increased public responsibilities that you will face
in our new life here.
  Vanessa is probably right about waiting until March
to put the house on the market. That way we can have
any repairs done, and you can take your time sorting
through everything. I don't want you to feel stressed
out. River Oaks does look its best in March with all
the azaleas blooming everywhere. Anyone on a
househunting trip from the North wouldn't be able to
resist it. And we know that March and April are the
recruiting months in Houston.
  When you are sorting out my closet, don't throw
away my Stanford sweatshirt. I know that you think it
is old and ratty, but I think that it is just broken
in.
  Julia has been introducing me to all her big donor
friends in Boston. This Saturday I am going with her
to the Opera Guild Ball.
  Kiss the kids for me.
  I wish you were here in my arms.
  Love Bob

Today I helped with an art project in Susan's class. We have such a great school. I feel lucky that Alex and Susan can go there, but of course that is why we chose this neighborhood. I hopethat we can find a school like this in Massachusetts.

Anna played with Susan after school. Anna's dad was outoftown, so I invited Anna and her mom to stay for dinner. Meredith is so nice, too bad she is so busy all the time with her two older boys soccerteams.

The Wentworth Heart Institute

Spring Gala

Dinner and Dan

Saturda

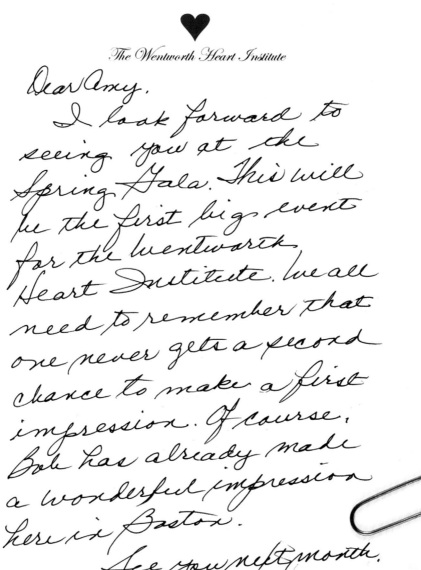

The Wentworth Heart Institute

Dear Amy,

I look forward to seeing you at the Spring Gala. This will be the first big event for the Wentworth Heart Institute. We all need to remember that one never gets a second chance to make a first impression. Of course, Bob has already made a wonderful impression here in Boston.

See you next month.

Julia

Parent volunteer, Amy Mason helps third grade students with an art project.

Parent Volunteers Make Our School Great

River Oaks Elementary School can thank much of its great success to the wonderful parent volunteers who spend countless hours

n Commons, Swan boats

POST CARD

Dear Susan and Alex,
    Thanks for emailing
your letters and drawings.
Alex, That looks just like
me.
    I'm sorry that I'll miss
your piano recital on
Thursday but it's nice that
Miss Vanessa can go with
Mommy. I know you
will have fun at the
Dessert Gallery after
the recital! I wish
I was There.
Kiss Mommy for me
        Love, Daddy

The Masons
2609 Violet Lane
Houston, Tx. 77019

friday
CO#1283

Now it broadly takes
Now the wharves upon th
Lessening, leave us by degr
Blithely blow the

Lemon-Green Olive Salsa

We like to make this when we have grilled tuna.

1 cup green olives
2 tablespoons capers, rinsed
2 lemons
1/2 cup pine nuts
1/3 cup olive oil

Coarsely chop the olives. Slice the peel off the lemons. Coarsely chop the lemons, retaining juice. Mix olives, lemons, lemon juice, pinenuts, capers and olive oil.

Spoon over grilled fish.

Seem'd to fill with the eyes' light, like some ruin'd
    fountain
Everlasting and wisdom far off as the mountain
That gazing in a garden desert of its streams,
And still the more lovely its loneliness seems.
So that, watching that face, you could scarce pause
    to guess
The years which its calm careworn lines might express,
Feeling only what suffering with these must have past
To have perfected there so much sweetness at last.

                         XV.

Thus, one bronzed evening, when day had put out
His brief thrifty fires, and the wind was about,
The nun, watchful still by the boy, on his own
Laid a firm quiet hand, and the deep tender tone
Of her voice moved the silence.   She said . . . 'I have heal'd
'These wounds of the body. Why hast thou conceal'd,
'Young soldier, that yet open wound in the heart?
'Wilt thou trust no hand near it?'
                         He winced, with a start,
As one that is suddenly touch'd on the spot
From which every nerve derives suffering.
                                         'What?
Thou here, too, then, so bare?' he moan'd bitterly.
                                         'Nay,'
With passionate accents she hasten'd to say,
'Do you think that these eyes are with sorrow, young
    man,
'So all but blinded, as to scan
'Her features, . . . view them not?
                         'Oh! was it spoken,
'"Go ye forth, heal the sick, and . . . bind the
    broken!"
'Of the body alone is our mission then, done,
'When we leave the bruised spirits, if we bind the
    bruised bone?
'Nay, is not the mission of mercy two-fold

Lived there ... any lands in the fa...
Say, O friend, if ... evening thou c...
Some pale and ... available vapour,
From the ... and disconsolate earth, ... fall
O'er the ... of a sweet serene star, until all
The mild ... splendour reluctantly waned in the deep
Of its own native heaven? From so seem'd to creep
O'er that fair and ... by day,
While the radiant ve... away,
Hid its light in the hea... gradual veil
Of a sadness unconscious ... grew pale
As silent her lord gre... they eyed
Each the other askan... secretly sigh'd.
Ah, wise friend, what ... rience can give?
True, we know what li... as! do we live?
The grammar of life w... by heart,
But life's self we have ... language—an art
Not a voice.   Co... once, as 'twas
  spoken
When the silenc... was broken!
Cuvier knew the... no doubt:
But the last ma... about
What the first, ... What art
  thou
To the man of t...
  science.   Wh... from ocean
First beheld the... n emotion!
When life leap... b... ts in the
  heart,
When it thrills as ... part,
Where lurks it? how works it? . . we scarcely detect
  it.
But life goes: the heart dies: haste, O leech, and di...
  sect it!
This accursed æsthetical, ethical age
Hath so fingered life's horn-book, so blurr'd every page,
That the old ... romance, the gay chivalrous story
With its fables of faery, its legends of glory,
Is turn'd to a tedious instruction, not new

Hi Bob,
It's midnight on Sunday and I'm feeling lonely. I
didn't want to call you because it's so late.

What a wonderful Saturday we had. I feel like the
character in "Rebecca" who says "I wish there could be
an invention that bottled up the memory like perfume
and it never faded... Then whenever I wanted to, I
could uncork the bottle and, live the memory all over
again."

If I could I would bottle up last Saturday--what a
lovely, perfect day. Our lazy morning, with Alex and
Susan jumping into our bed for a family cuddle, the
wonderful lunch on the patio at El Pueblito, the
stroll around the Bayou Bend gardens, and the nice
dinner on our patio. All in all, a perfect day. I will
try to bottle it up and remember it when I am feeling
depressed and lonely.

It was so nice of you to offer to take the kids and do
the shopping for dinner. I really enjoyed my soak in
the tub, but I have to admit I was a little annoyed
that when you ran into Vanessa at Central Market, you
invited her to join us for dinner. I was looking
forward to just family. But it turned out fine. She is
very interesting and I think that she really likes the
kids. When Vanessa and I were in the kitchen, I was
surprised that she said she envies me, that I have it
all, with such a great husband, beautiful children and
great life. I know how happy I am with our life, but I
didn't think that I have the kind of life that a woman
like Vanessa would envy. I thought that she would find
my life pretty boring.

I have to start planning for my trip to Boston for the
Spring Gala. I need to arrange for someone to stay
with the children. That will be hard, because we
always depended on Mom, and I am not sure who to call.
I may ask Alex's teacher, Miss Thompson. Susan and
Alex both love her. I hope she can do it. I also need
to find a suitable dress--you know how I hate
shopping. I am dreading that. I'm not even sure what I
should be looking for.
Love Amy

I can't wait to see Bob in Boston, but I wish that we could spend the weekend alone. I hope that ~~Bob~~ Mrs. Wentworth won't be disappointed in me. I am never comfortable at big parties. I never know what to say.

From: "Bob Mason" <mason2609@yahoo.com>

Subject: Re: Our weekend

To: amyzmason@yahoo.com

Amy,

It was a nice weekend.
You should ask Vanessa about where to go for a dress.
She would know, because she attends lots of formal
occasions and fundraisers. Speaking of fundraising, it
would probably be helpful for you to pick her brain
for ideas that we might use here.
Kiss the kids for me. Wish you were here.
Bob

Woman. It left on his senses the delicious
perfume so familiar as Lavinia's favorite long ago,
and recalled the past like a withered flower given
as a token by a beloved hand. It seem
wholly represented to

Lightly
Ready
Which

From: "Amy Mason" <amyzmason@yahoo.com>

Subject: Our day

To: mason2609@yahoo.com

Hi Bob,

Hope you had a good time this evening at the fundraiser. I won't call now because it's so late. Call me tomorrow morning. I miss you.

I took the car for an oil change this afternoon. It ended up taking way longer than I expected. I was just starting to panic about being late to pick the kids up at school when Vanessa called me on my cell phone. She was so nice, she said that she was working at home and she could easily go across the street and pick up the kids. They could visit her until I came by to get them. Luckily the women in the school office all know me and I was able to give permission for Vanessa to pick up Susan and Alex. All this time that I have seen that luxury high rise across the street from the school, I never imagined that our kids would go there after school to play!

I got there about 4:30. All I can say is WOW! What a place! The view from Vanessa's apartment is amazing! I was surprised that she had such a large place, but she told me that she was able to buy the condo for an unbelievable price after the Enron collapse. It looks like something out of "Architectural Digest."

Vanessa had a telescope in her livingroom, and when she went to tell the kids to gather up the things in her den, I looked through it. You won't believe what I could see--Our patio! I was shocked, because without the telescope, our neighborhood looks like all trees. I never imagined that someone in this building could see us! It made me feel funny, I always thought of our patio as a very private place. Vanessa came back into the room and I guess she could tell I was surprised. She said that the kids were trying to see if they could pick out our house.

Vanessa said that the brochures were almost ready and that she has scheduled the agent open house.

Susan and Alex came running into the livingroom (that place has probably never had kids running around in it before). I was a little worried, but Vanessa seemed comfortable with them. They wanted to be sure that I saw all the rooms. I can see Susan adjusting to that lifestyle easily!! She was very impressed by it all.

We miss you,
Love Amy

Dear Amy,
That must have been fun for the kids to see Vanessa's place. I don't think that they have ever been in a high rise condo before.

I am also surprised that you could see our patio. But since we can see the top few floors of the Huntington from the patio, I guess it makes sense.

I am sorry that I can't make it home this weekend. We are so busy.
Kiss the kids for me.
Bob

support.
paced he the murmurous pathways where myrtles,
court up to court,
th roses in garden on garden, were ranged
d fountains that fed
l music green odorous twilights: and so,
lifting his head
p from the way he walked wearily, he to the
se of Pride
ded, and

In clus
Burning inward and onward, from
down distances vast
tuous vistas, illumined
se silentness passed
mon sighing; where col
red in groves
es of the forest in L
wind, as it moves,
rs, "I, too, am Solom
runks hid in garlands of g
whose tops the skill'd sc
granted men's gaze to beh
How the phenix that sits on th
'mid fragrance and fire,
dying, and living, hath
funeral pyre;
stork builds her nes
the palm-branc
oe's great blosso
the life that it en

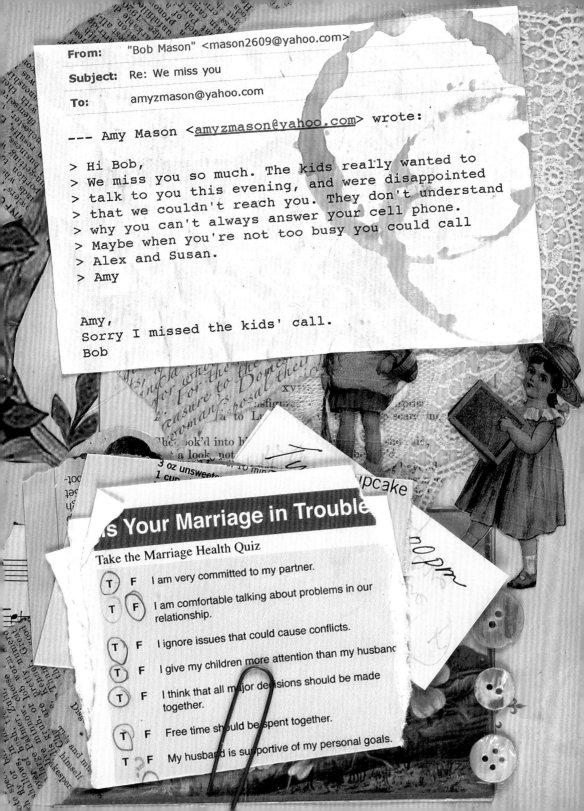

From: "Bob Mason" <mason2609@yahoo.com>

Subject: Re: We miss you

To: amyzmason@yahoo.com

--- Amy Mason <amyzmason@yahoo.com> wrote:

> Hi Bob,
> We miss you so much. The kids really wanted to
> talk to you this evening, and were disappointed
> that we couldn't reach you. They don't understand
> why you can't always answer your cell phone.
> Maybe when you're not too busy you could call
> Alex and Susan.
> Amy

Amy,
Sorry I missed the kids' call.
Bob

Is Your Marriage in Trouble

Take the Marriage Health Quiz

(T) F I am very committed to my partner.

T (F) I am comfortable talking about problems in our relationship.

(T) F I ignore issues that could cause conflicts.

(T) F I give my children more attention than my husband

(T) F I think that all major decisions should be made together.

(T) F Free time should be spent together.

T F My husband is supportive of my personal goals.

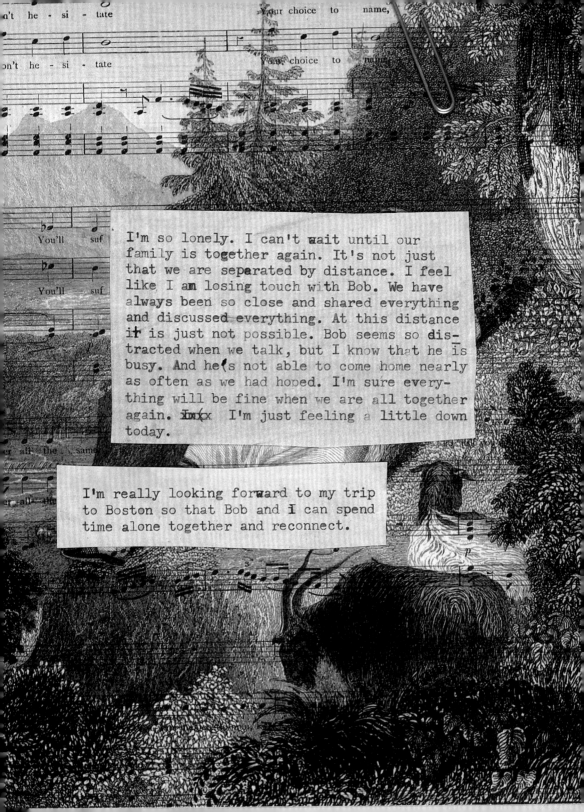

I'm so lonely. I can't wait until our family is together again. It's not just that we are separated by distance. I feel like I am losing touch with Bob. We have always been so close and shared everything and discussed everything. At this distance it is just not possible. Bob seems so distracted when we talk, but I know that he is busy. And he's not able to come home nearly as often as we had hoped. I'm sure everything will be fine when we are all together again. I~~mxx~~ I'm just feeling a little down today.

I'm really looking forward to my trip to Boston so that Bob and I can spend time alone together and reconnect.

From: "Amy Mason" <amyzmason@yahoo.com>

Subject: Hi

To: mason2609@yahoo.com

Hi,
It was really great to talk to you last night. I guess I have just been feeling really lonely for the last few days and I have had such trouble sleeping.

The field trip with Alex's class was fun, and I think that he was proud to have his mom along. Vanessa stopped by again tonight. It was such a lovely evening that we had a glass of wine out on the patio. She is so easy to talk to, and I told her about my sleep problems. She suggested that I take something to help me sleep. I don't like the idea of taking drugs. I don't know what to do. I really do need a good night's sleep.

Vanessa happened to see the clipping of you and Mrs. Wentworth. Vanessa said that she'd be worried if she had a good looking husband who spent so much time with an attractive, wealthy widow.

Should I be worried? lol
Love Amy

'Yes! yes!
'That is too true indeed!' . . . the Duke sigh'd.

From: "Bob Mason" <mason2609@yahoo.com>

Subject: Re: Hi

To: "Amy Mason" <amyzmason@yahoo.com>

A--
Ha,Ha, she's old enough to be my mother!
B.

'One pang of wrong d'love, to which women less ful
'Are exposed, when they love?'

From: "Amy Mason" <amyzmason@yahoo.com>

Subject: Re: Re: Hi

To: mason2609@yahoo.com

Bob,
Pretty glamorous mother!!!
Amy

CANTO I.]

' So excited,
' Throughou
   grow—
' Those eloq
' Which that
(He pointed
Fixing with
' Have you
   view
' In that fac
' Young, lov
' Are you lo

The grou
   spoke
This close.

Julia Wentworth and Dr. Robert Mason

Opera Guild Ball

It was all glamour and glitter last night at the 48th annual Opera Guild Ball. Those in attendance included Julia Wentworth, escorted by the new director of the Wentworth Heart Institute, Dr. Robert Mason. Mrs. Wentworth wore
Chanel evening dress and her heirloom

From:	"Bob Mason"
Subject:	Re: Re: Hi
To:	amyzmason@yahoo.com

Amy,
I'm sorry that you're still not sleeping well. You know that I'm not the type of Doc who thinks prescriptions are the answer to everything, but in this case Vanessa could be right. Sleep deprivation can be very serious. I think that you should give Jim a call and ask him to prescribe something. I am sure that after a few good nights of sleep, things will look a lot brighter.
Love,
Bob

Grant-Garamond Realty

A rare opportunity to acquire this prestigious River Oaks property on coveted Violet Lane. This charming four bedroom, four bath home has been beautifully updated. On a large lot, with an enchanting private walled garden.

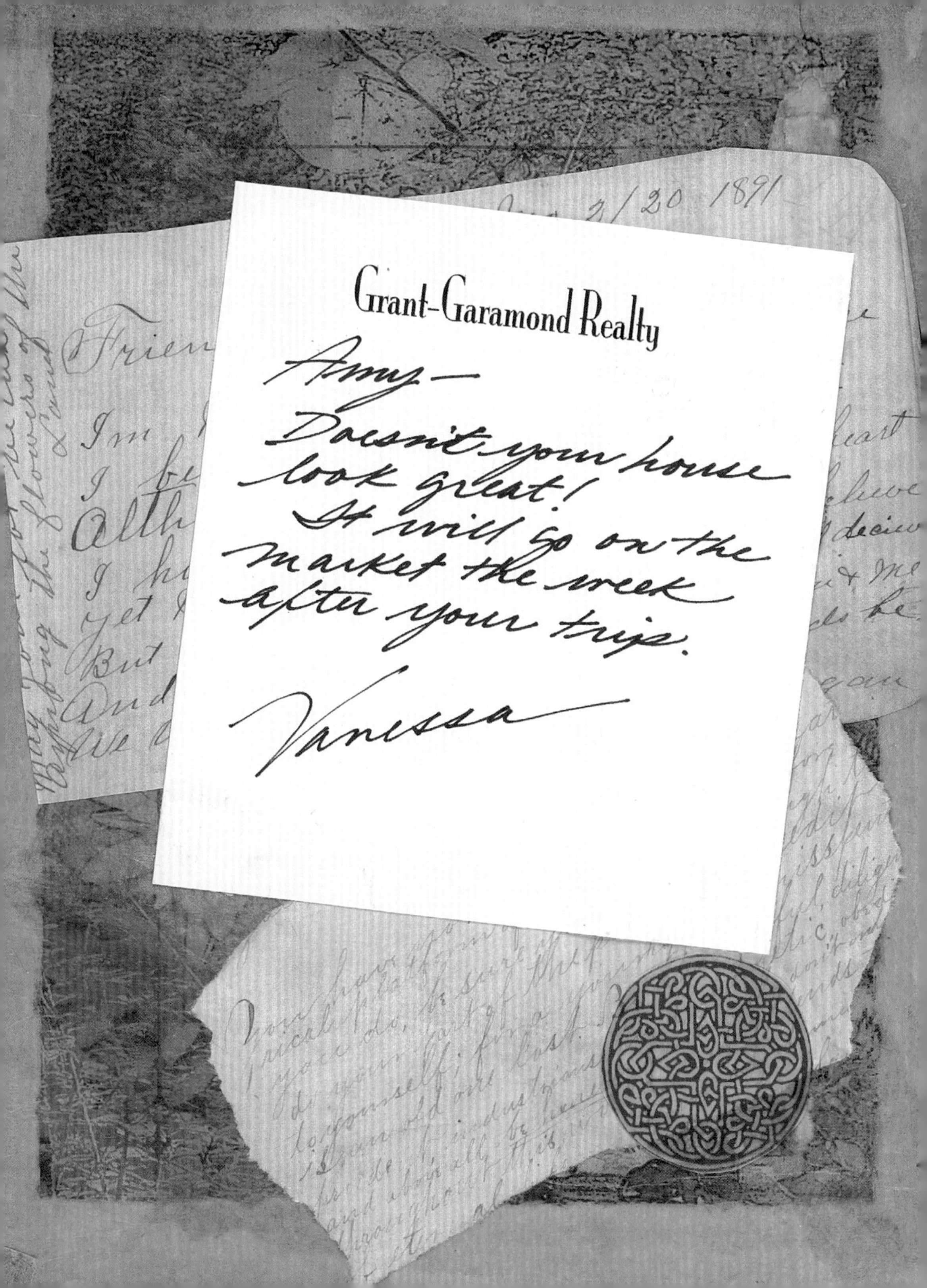
Grant-Garamond Realty
Amy—
Doesn't your house look great!
It will go on the market the week after your trip.
Vanessa

Beat the Blues

- Think positive thoughts
- Accept yourself
- Express your feeli...
- Cultivate...dsh...
- Get a...

Some Jade Gar...

Chinese Resta...

Dine In • Take-out • C...

APPETIZERS

...gg Roll (2)
...ried Wonton (12)
...ho-Cho Beef (6)
...parerib (8)
...team or Fried Dump...
...ried Shrimp (6)

Place the pep...

3 cup to...
3 large ga...
¼ cup extr...
3 tablespoo...
or 1 to 2 ou...
blespoons)

order new
stationery
Cathy K. Butler
www.acutesite.com
505~98...
acutesit...

Rebecca
1:00pm
Tuesday

...ility to sense and
...th.
...5

OFFICE HOURS
BY APPOINTMENT

DR. REBECCA BRENNER, M.D.

PSYCHIATRY

1600 Me...

False friends are worst than bitter enemies

...cup silvered...
...cup olive oil...

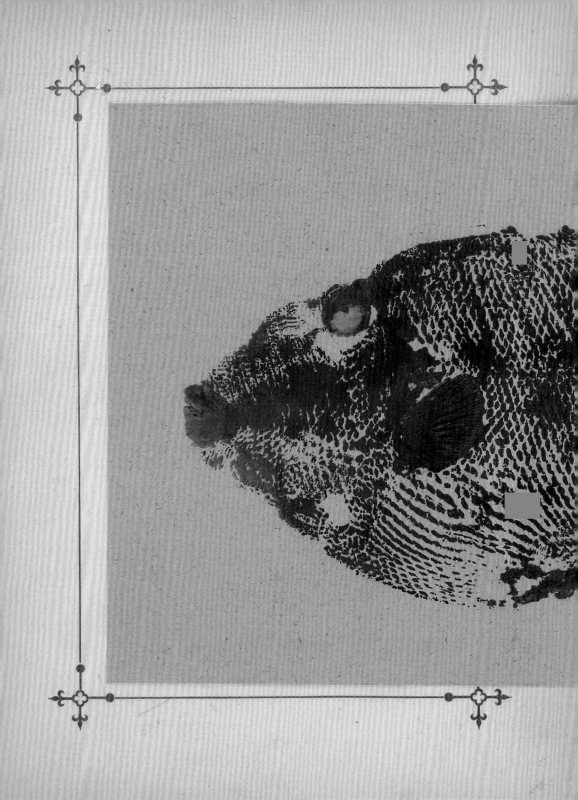

From: "Amy Mason" <amyzmason@yahoo.com>

Subject: Hi Daddy

To: mason2609@yahoo.com

Dear Daddy,
How come you didn't come home this weekend? I miss
you. We went to the art museum today with Miss
Vanessa. I love Miss Vanessa. She is so pretty and
nice. Mommy and Alex and Miss Vanessa and me learned
how to do gyotaku. I bet you don't know what that is.
It was fun but sort of gross.
Love and lots of kisses, Susan

He had thought, too, of glory, and fortune, and power:

Hi Susie-Q

I really miss you too. I couldn't come home this
weekend because I had to go to some important
meetings, but I'll come home for a visit as soon as I
can.

I am glad that you had so much fun on Saturday with
Miss Vanessa. She is very pretty and nice. I will
guess what gyotaku is--is it an Asian dance?

I miss you, kiss Mommy and Alex for me,
Daddy

Dear Daddy,
You are silly. Gyotaku isn't a dance. Gyo means fish
and taku means impression. We made fish impressions.
You get a dead fish and put paint on it and use it
like a rubber stamp. It was cool and gross.
Vanessa loved the picture I made. I gave it to her and
she said that she would frame it and hang it in her
cool house. I made another one for you. I know you
love to eat fish.
love Susan

From: "Amy Mason" <amyzmason@yahoo.com>

Subject: Hi

To: mason2609@yahoo.com

Dear Bob,

    I see that Susan has written to you about our fun Saturday. Vanessa is so nice. She knew we were sad about not seeing you for a couple of weeks, so she surprised us by planning a great day. Vanessa told the kids that she had something "fishy" planned. And did she ever!

    First we went to the museum and as Susan told you, we learned "gyotaku". I enjoyed it as much as the kids did. And the results were beautiful. Wait until you see our pictures.

    Next we went to the Downtown Aquarium. The kids loved it. We went through all the exhibits and Vanessa treated us to lunch at the restaurant. She arranged for us to have a table right next to one of the big windows into the aquarium. It was spectacular.

    For dessert we went to The Chocolate Bar. After we ate our great dessert, Vanessa bought Susan and Alex chocolate fish. I think that Vanessa is now Alex and Susan's favorite person!

    The fun continued when we got home. Vanessa gave the children a present. It was "The Little Mermaid". While the kids watched the movie, Vanessa and I opened a bottle of wine and sat out on the patio. It was nice talking to an adult. It was a lovely day.

    We miss you. Call when you get a chance.

    Love, Amy

That heaves the happy sea:

Amy,

Sounds like you had a great time. Sorry I missed it. That was really great of Vanessa, considering that Saturday must be one of her busiest days. I'll have to call and thank her for being such a good friend to my family. That was something to have the whole day planned around a theme. She's very creative.

Vanessa has become such a family friend that I know that you, Susan and Alex will miss her when we move. But she says that she loves Boston. Who knows, maybe she'll end up here one day.

Julia has taken me to some fantastic restaurants. We'll have to try some when you get here.
Kiss the kids for me,
Bob

Life's truest happiness is found in friendships we make along the way.

Friendship without self-interest is one of the rare and beautiful things of life.

think this is the beginning of a beautiful friendship

Friendship is one mind in two bodies.

Friends are treasures.

Friendship improves happiness, and abates misery, by doubling our joys, and dividing our grief.

I am surprised how quickly Vanessa and I have become friends.
When we moved to Houston, the kids were so young and with Bob
and Mom, I felt that my life was full. I realize that I didn't
feel the need to cultivate friendships. Now with Mom gone and
Bob up in Boston and the kids in school all day, I am feeling

a gap in my life. Luckily, I met Vanessa or I'd feel even more
lonely right now. When we move to Massachusetts, I will make an
effort to become involved in our new community. I know that I
will volunteer in the children's school, and I will meet people
there. I think that I will also look for some sort of art group
and hope to find friends who share my interests.

From: "Amy Mason" <amyzmason@yahoo.com>

Subject: My trip

To: mason2609@yahoo.com

Hi Bob,

    I think that I have it all arranged for my trip to Boston for the Spring Gala. Everything but the dress. I made my plane reservations to leave Friday at 10 am and be back home Monday at 1:00 pm. Alex's teacher, Miss Thompson said that she would love to come and stay with the children for the weekend.

    I have an appointment with Vanessa's hair stylist for Thursday afternoon. Vanessa's hair always looks so great, I'll see what he can do for me. Vanessa asked what color I used on my hair and she was surprised when I told her that it was my natural color.

    Now I just have to find a dress.

    Love, Amy

But the great fact of my own pain: I saw
    I heard the cries:
The crow's shade dwindled up the hill

Amy

I'm glad Miss Thompson can stay with the kids. They like her. I have the weekend planned. I booked a suite at the Ritz-Carlton, so we won't have to drive since the ball is there. We can househunt a little on Saturday and Sunday. I found some areas that I really like.

And don't change the color of your hair. You know that's why I fell in love with you. lol
Bob

From: "Amy Mason" <amyzmason@yahoo.com>

Subject: Re: Re: My trip

To: mason2609@yahoo.com

Dear Bob,

 I'm so excited, I can't wait--a luxurious weekend, just the two of us. Let's have room service breakfast in bed on Saturday.

 Vanessa has been such a good friend. My hair appointment is at 2:30 on Thursday afternoon and Vanessa said that she would pick up Alex and Susan at school and give them dinner. I'll have lots of time to get ready.

 Can't wait! Love,
Amy

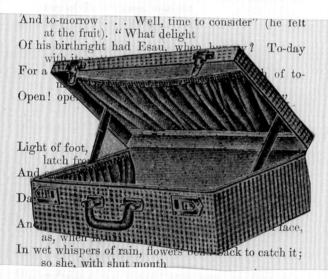

And to-morrow . . . Well, time to consider" (he felt
 at the fruit). "What delight
Of his birthright had Esau, when h▢▢▢▢? To-day
 with its ▢▢▢
For a ▢▢▢▢▢▢▢▢▢▢▢▢▢h of to-
 ▢▢
Open! ope▢▢▢▢▢▢▢▢▢▢▢▢▢"

Light of foot, ▢▢▢▢
 latch fr▢▢
And ▢▢▢

Da▢▢

An▢▢▢▢▢▢▢▢▢▢▢▢▢▢▢▢ ace,
as, when ▢▢▢▢
In wet whispers of rain, flowers b▢▢▢back to catch it;
 so she, with shut mouth

 Vanessa says that this is my chance to prove myself in Boston. She says that I should just be myself, and not be nervous.

VALUES IN SUMMER FROCKS

VALUE.

DELIGHTFUL SUMMER FROCKS

I found the perfect dress for the Ball. I'm really proud because I found it myself. Instead of going to the stores that Vanessa recommended, I went to a vintage shop and found a beautiful vintage Givenchy. It is simple and elegant and it makes me feel like Audrey Hepburn.

the fairest of blossom from Friend

"BASLOW."

Alex is so sick. I can't believe that this happened.
I was looking forward to my trip so much. But I
shouldn't be thinking of myself when Alex is so
sick. I feel sad for Bob too. When I called him
to tell him that I couldn't come, he sounded so
~~angry~~ disappointed, and also concerned for Alex.

When I picked up Susan and Alex at Vanessa's
last night, everything seemed fine. Vanessa
had given them dinner so I would have more time
to get ready for the trip. About an hour after
Alex went to bed he woke up crying. He felt so
sick, with a stomach ache and vomiting. He
couldn't keep anything down. I was getting worried
so I called Bob. I was glad when he said that he
would call Jim and ask him to come ~~over~~ over and
look at Alex. Jim is so nice. He came over right
away. I am glad that he lives so close to us.
Jim thought that it was something that Alex ate.
He questioned Alex and Susan about whatthey had
that afternoon and evening. Susan said that she
and Alex ate all the same things at Vanessa's,
but luckily Susan isn't sick too. I tried to call
Vanessa but I can't reach her. Jim gave Alex something to settle his stomach. Alex was awake most
of the night, but now he's finally sleeping. He
seems to be over the worst of it, but obviously
he won't be well enough for me to go on the trip.

And he sleeps, he

From: "Bob Mason" <mason2609@yahoo.com>

Subject: Call me when you get this

To: amyzmason@yahoo.com

Amy--
I didn't want to call and risk waking up Alex. If you
get this, call me right away. You won't believe what
happened this evening.
I hope Alex is feeling better.
Bob

From: "Bob Mason" <mason2609@yahoo.com>

Subject: News

To: amyzmason@yahoo.com

Amy,
It's 2:00 am. I guess you're not online and it's too
late to call, but I can't wait to tell you what
happened this evening.

I went to the ball, a little depressed because you
weren't here and I was worried about Alex, but I knew
that I had to make an appearance. I was walking
through the lobby on the way to the ballroom when I
felt a tap on my shoulder. You won't believe who it
was--Vanessa! For a minute I looked at this beautiful
woman, not registering who she was because it was so
unexpected. She said that she was in Boston to attend
a wedding Saturday afternoon, which coincidentally was
at the Ritz-Carlton. She was so shocked and upset
when I told her that you weren't here and that Alex
had been so sick. She knew how much you were looking
forward to the trip. Vanessa is so kind. She said that
she would give anything if she could switch places
with you and take care of Alex for us.

Since the wedding had just finished and I was on my
own, I had the great idea of asking her to go with me
to the ball. At first she said no, but I talked her
into it. I knew that Julia would love to meet someone
with Vanessa's fundraising experience. I was right.
She and Julia really hit it off. Vanessa is so
charming and vivacious.

Julia wanted to talk to Vanessa in depth, so she
invited us to brunch tomorrow morning.
Hope Alex is feeing better.

With her life was at war. Once, but once, in that life
The chance had been hers to escape from this strife
In herself; finding peace in the life of another
From the passionate wants she, in hers, fail'd to
     smother.
But the chance fell too soon, when the crude restless
     power
Which had been to her nature so fatal a dower,
Only wearied the man it yet haunted and thrall'd;
And that moment, once past, had been never recall'd.
Yet it left her heart sore; and, to shelter her heart
From approach, she then sought, in that delicate art
Of concealment, those thousand adroit strategies
Of feminine wit, which repel while they please,
A weapon, at once, and a shield, to conceal
And defend all that women can earnestly feel.
Thus, striving her instincts to hide and repress,
She felt frighten'd at times by her very success;
She pined for the hill-tops, the clouds, and the stars:
Golden wires may annoy us as much as steel bars
If they keep us behind prison-windows: impassion'd
Her heart rose and burst the light cage she had
     fashion'd
Out of glittering trifles around it.

                          Unknown
To herself, all her instincts, without hesitation,
Embraced the idea of self-immolation.
The strong spirit in her, had her life but been founded
With some man whose heart had her own apprehended,
     hended,
All its wealth at his feet would have lavishly thrown.
For him she had struggled and striven alone;
For him had toil'd; in him had transfused
All the gladness and grace of her nature; and used
For him only the spells of its delicate power:
Like the ministering fairy that brings from her bower
To some mage all the treasures, whose use the fond
     elf,
More enrich'd by her love, disregards for herself.
But standing apart, as she ever had done,

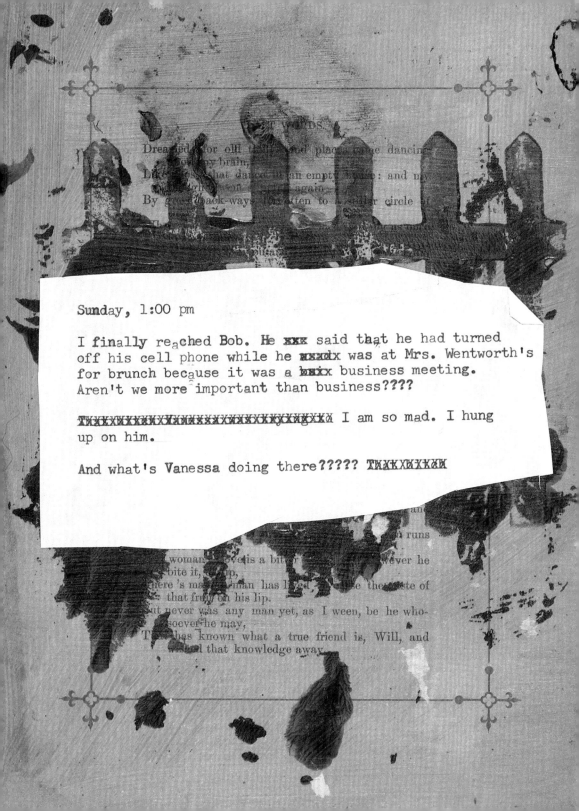

Sunday, 1:00 pm

I finally re_ached Bob. He ~~xxx~~ said that he had turned
off his cell phone while he ~~xxxdx~~ was at Mrs. Wentworth's
for brunch because it was a ~~bxix~~ business meeting.
Aren't we more important than business????

~~XXXXXXXXXXXXXXXXXXXXXXXXXXXXXX~~ I am so mad. I hung
up on him.

And what's Vanessa doing there????? ~~TXXXXXXXXXX~~

Absence makes the heart grow fonder.

Lucile.—Page 170.

3:00 pm   I just had a long talk with Vanessa and Bob. Maybe
I am feeling a little better. I don't know what to think. I
was so upset and angry. ~~xxxxIxhavexxxrightxtoxbex~~ Maybe I was
over-reacting and jumping to conclusions. Vanessa said that
Bob was so worried about how angry I was. ~~DxxxtxxIxhavexxxright~~
She said that he is missing me so much and is so ~~xxxxxrxxdxxbxt~~
concerned about me and Alex. He can't stand the thought of
how disappointed I must be about ~~mixix~~ missing the trip.

Vanessa explained that she had planned her trip to Boston
several months ago. She didn't want to mention it when she
realized that we would be in Boston at the same time and
~~xxx~~ even ~~xx~~ at the same hotel, because she knew how much I
was looking forward to spending time alone with Bob. Vanessa
said ~~thxtxshexdidnt~~ that she didn't want anything to interfer
with that. She thinks that we ~~xxxxx~~ are so nice and ~~ixx~~ if
we knew that she was in Boston we would invite her to dinner
or something. Bob said that Vanessa was just trying to be
thoughtful by not mentioning her trip.

She offered to go househunting with Bob this afternoon. I
guess it will be helpful to have her point of view and
Bob seems ~~xx~~ happy to haveher along since she is a real
estate agent.

I was so mad, but I guess it all makes sense. I am calmer
now. I did call the Ritz-Carlton in Boston. There was a
wedding there on Saturday afternoon.

Yet there's none so unhappy, but what he hath been
Just about to be happy, at some time, I ween;

Subject: Hello darling

To: amyzmason@yahoo.com

Amy,

I'm so glad that we talked this afternoon and that you talked with Vanessa and everything is cleared up. I understand how upsetting this weekend has been for you. I am glad that Alex is so much better. He sounded great on the phone.

I don't want you to worry about missing the gala. It actually went well. Julia enjoyed meeting Vanessa and was thrilled to hear about her extensive fundraising experience. Julia said that someone like Vanessa would be such an asset to the Institute. I'm glad that you and Vanessa are friends, because you can learn a lot from her. I hadn't actually realized just how much Julia expects from the Director's wife.

I know that you must be exhausted after staying up several nights with Alex. I hope that you can get a good night's sleep.

Bob

'I entreat, I conjure you, by all that you feel
'Or profess, to come to me directly.
                                              'LUCILE.'

Subject: Househunting

To: amyzmason@yahoo.com

Amy,
Vanessa and I saw some interesting open houses. I really learned a lot househunting with her. She knows just what to ask about each house.

I've attached a link to some of the houses that we saw. You would like the one near Concord, but I am having second thoughts about a suburban location. Julia thinks that we should live in the city because it would be more practical for entertaining. It is something to think about.
Bob

Vanessa called today and asked if she could
come over and bring us dinner this evening along
with the information on houses in Massachusetts.
I know that it's not her fault, but I can't help
feeling a little resentful that she was the one who
spent time with Bob this weekend and helped look for
MY HOUSE. XXXXXXXXX I know I really should be happy
that she was able to help Bob look at houses. It made
it easier for him. XXXXxxxxke

I told Vanessa to come at six. She brought pizzas
from La Griglia and four different desserts. She
sure knows how to please Susan and Alex. She also
brought them gifts from her trip. Susan loved the
necklace but I told Alex that he could only try
using those juggling balls outside, never in the
house.
Vanessa brought the house brochures and notes on
each one that she and Bob visited. She does have
an eye for detail. I almost felt like I xxxx had
seen each house. Vanessa said that she was glad she
XXX was able to help out by accompanying Bob,
because he was so disappointed that I couldn't
be there. She told me all about the Gala and the
brunch at Julia's beautiful home. It seems that
everyone is very impressed with Bob. Vanessa said
how lucky I was--it would be very exciting to be
Bob's wife. And she really liked Julia. Vanessa is
looking forward to talking to Julia again with
ideas for the Institute's fundraising events.
I guess she and Julia really XXXXX hit it off.

So that thought more than once darken'd over his
    heart
For a moment, and rapidly seem'd to depart.

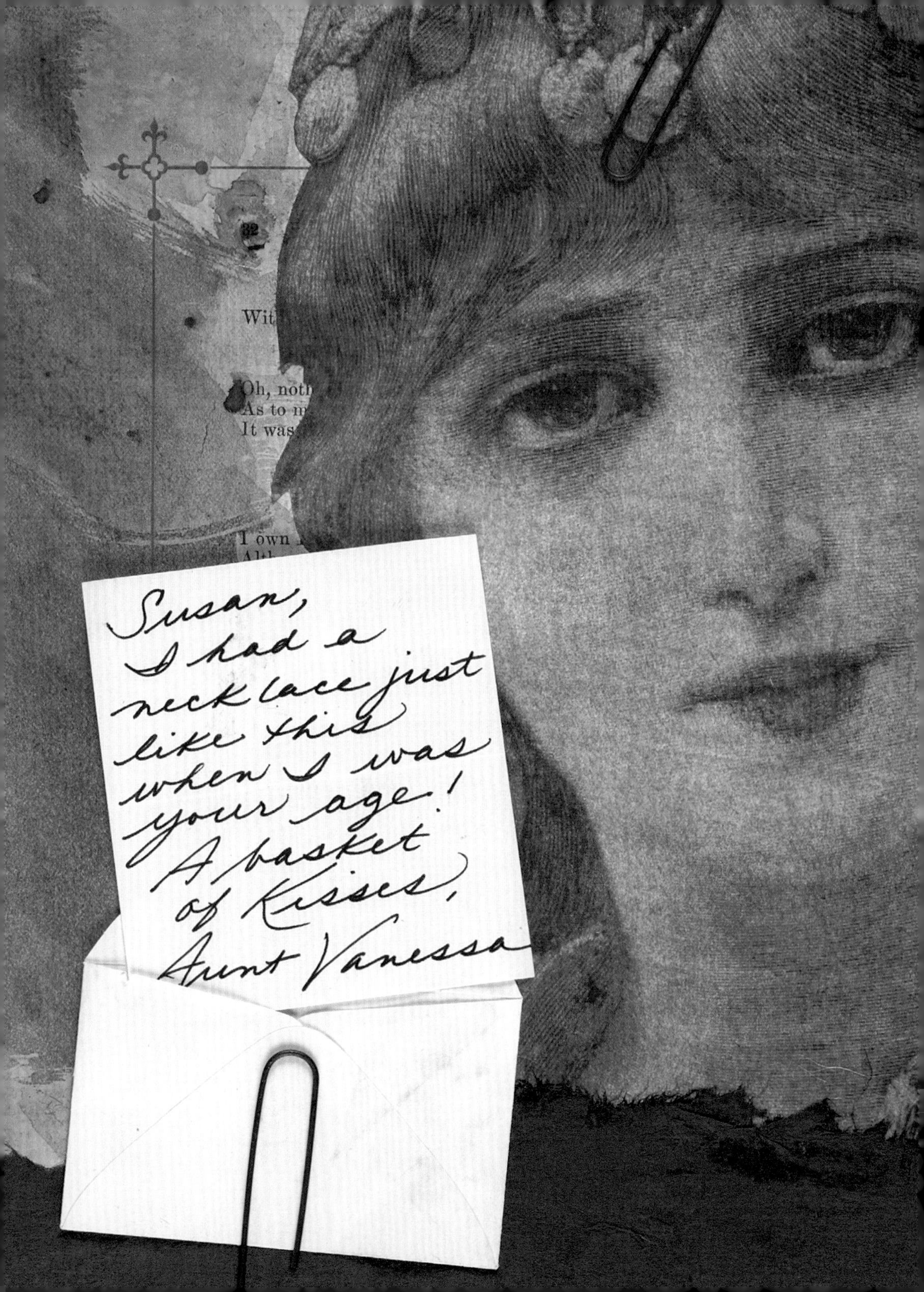
Susan,
I had a
necklace just
like this
when I was
your age!
A basket
of Kisses,
Aunt Vanessa

Historic Home Near Concord, M

Overlooking the Concord River, this circa 185 i
near Concord has been painstakingly restored
great attention to detail. Original wood floors
4 working fireplaces, 5 bedrooms, gathering ro
The recently renovated kitchen opens to the su
master suite with fireplace and sitting area. Li
and attic studio. 2.3 acres, beautifully landsca

Dear Mrs. M

It was so nice to
meet you and your
husband at the Open
House on Sunday.
You are such a
lovely couple. I would
enjoy working with you
(over)

Dear Bob,

Tomorrow the house officially goes on the market. I feel like all I have been doing is cleaning. But I feel so much better since I have been sleeping well the last few nights. I guess that I really did need something to help me sleep. My big challenge now will be to keep the house clean ALL THE TIME. I know that some real estate agents don't give much warning when they want to show the house. I have been trying to think of some fun places to take the kids on the spur of the moment when someone comes to see the house.

Mr. Momsen called from the bank. He wanted to talk to you about the details of transferring your 401K. I said that you'd give him a call. Susan got to bring home the class tree frog this weekend. Alex and Susan both loved having a pet, even just a frog. We will have to think about getting a dog when we move. They drew pictures of "Kermit" which I have scanned for you.

The children love getting your postcards. They don't take much time to write, you should send them more often.

I got a letter from a real estate agent in Concord, Abigail Williams. Did you like her? We do need an agent there. She is very eager to help us. By the way, she thought that you and Vanessa were Dr. and Mrs. Mason. She said that you made a lovely couple! I hope she won't be too disappointed when she meets the real Mrs. Mason!!!

We miss you. Call when you have time.

Love Amy

Attachment
alexfrog.jpg
.jpg file, 600x384, 34k

Attachment
Susanfrog.jpg
.jpg file, 600x857, 52k

His face, which was pale, gather'd force from the
glance.

Amy,
Sorry I'm not there to help with the house. I know
that you will be able to keep the kids busy with fun
activities. They always love the zoo.

I've been so busy with non-stop meetings this week.
I'll try to send more postcards. I'll ask Shirley to
pick up a supply next time she is out.

That real estate agent in Concord seemed fine. Vanessa
thought that she knew the suburban market very well,
but Julia recommended that we also work with an agent
that specializes in city properties.

Hope I can make it home the weekend after next. I will
try to call more often. Kiss the kids for me.

Bob

A lie born of that lying darkn...
Over all in his nature! He ar...
With a look which, if ever a m...
More intensely than words wh...
    vey'd
Beyond doubt in its smile an...

Mrs. Wentworth should NOT
be choosing where we live!
What about what is best for
Susan and Alex?? ~~Bob Should~~
~~tell Amxto~~

                    ll.

    And it bit, and it rankled.

From: "Amy Mason" <amyzmason@yahoo.com>

Subject: Open house a big success!!

To: mason2609@yahoo.com

Dear Bob,

The open house for the real estate agents was a big success. Vanessa was very happy with the positive feedback. She doesn't think that it will take long to sell the house. I had to be out of the house for a few hours so I spent it at Expo looking at dream kitchens.

The open house was over by the time I came back from picking up Susan and Alex at school. They thought that it looked like there had been a big party at our house. And it did. It was amazing how well we could see where everyone had walked on the freshly vacuumed carpet. When the carpet has just been vacuumed the foot impressions are so clear. The children were fascinated and followed the footprints around the house. Susan said that at least 3 people had gone in her closet!

Susan was invited for dinner at Anna's house. Anna is so sweet. Susan will really miss her when we move. I let Alex choose what he wanted for dinner, and of course he wanted a hamburger.

Call sometime. I hate to call you because it always seems like I'm interrupting something important, so call when you have a free minute.

Love

Amy

Our Open House

CANTO I.]   LUCILE.

JOHN.

                    One ...
Are you really in love with M...

ALFRED.

                              love, eh?
What a question!   Of course.

JOHN.

                    Were you really in love
With Madame de Ne...

                    ...But ... No, by Jove.

JOHN.

ALFRED.

                              Decidedly so.
...so she was some ten summers ago.
As soft and as sallow as Autumn—with hair
Neither black nor yet brown, but that bronze which one

...at eve in September, when night lingers long
...ugh a vineyard, with beams of a slow-setting sun.
...—the ... gazelle's; the fine foot ...
...A fay's ... to ... white and airy;
A voice soft ... some tune that one knows.
Something ... there was, set you thinking of those
Strange backgrounds of Raphael ... that hectic and
deep
...in which southern suns fall asleep.

JOHN.

...ette?

Dr. James Evans, Vanessa Garamond, Julia Wentworth and Dr. Robert Mason attend The Wentworth Institute Spring Gala.

From the pop of the first champagne cork, there was much to celebrate at the first annual Spring Gala for The Wentworth Heart Institute. The black tie event was held at the recently renovated Ritz-Carlton. Institute founder, **Julia Wentworth**, along with co-chairs **Denise Evans** and **Sophia Adams** hosted a dazzling evening of dining and dancing. Guests entered an enchanted wonderland of spring blossoms in the grand ballroom. Among those in attendance were newly appointed Wentworth Heart Institute Director, **Dr. Robert Mason** and his lovely guest, **Vanessa Garamond**, who came from Houston for the event. Also on hand were **Dr. and Mrs. Thomas Roland, Dr. and Mrs. Daniel Hemmingson, Liam and Lisa Owens, Lee and Ellen Patricks,** Institute Assistant Director, **Dr. Linda Miller**, and of course, husbands of the Gala co-chairs, **Dr. James Evans** and **Dr. Michael Adams**. Other out of town guests included **Robert and Cynthia Plain** of Virginia, **Dr. Brian and Dr. Astrid Meldrum** of London, D_ _ _ _ _ of Vancouver, _ _ _ _

FORWARD: Dr. John _ _ and Emma Parker-Jones

♥

The Wentworth Heart Institute

Mrs. Mason,

    Dr. Mason asked me to send you these insurance forms.

    Also I have en- closed some clippings that I thought you might like to see.

           Shirley

'How blind are you men!' she replied. 'Can you
    doubt
'That a woman, young, fair, and neglected—'
                        'Speak out!'
'He gasped with emotion. 'Lucile! you mean—what?
'Do you doubt her fidelity?'
                  'Certainly not.
'Listen to me, my friend.   What I wish to explain
'Is so hard to shape forth.   I could almost refrain

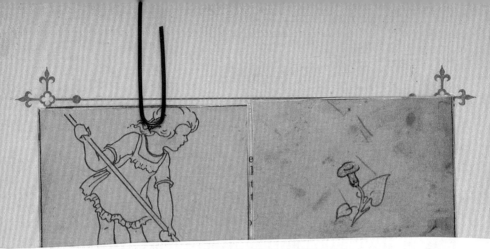

From:	"Amy Mason" <amyzmason@yahoo.com>
Subject:	Hi Daddy
To:	mason2609@yahoo.com

Dear Daddy,
I love you. I miss you. I love my new camera. I have
taken lots of pictures. I am sending you a funny one
that I took of Mommy through the window at Starbucks.
Mommy said that it looked artistic. I think I will be
an artist when I grow up.

I can't wait til you come home. I will take your
picture.

A basket of kisses
Susan

Franklin Park Zoo, Boston, Massachusetts

Franklin Park Zoo, Boston

USA 37

Amy,
I'm glad that I got to talk to the kids before they
were asleep. Susan now thinks that she's a detective.
She told me in great detail about all the footprints
around the house. She could tell where everyone went,
and that she knew that most were women because the
high heels leave a funny print.

When I told Susan that I have their frog pictures
hanging in my office, she was very proud. Alex wasn't
as impressed.

I had a long talk with Vanessa about the real estate
market in Boston and particular parts of the city. She
said that she would do a some research and get back to
me. Vanessa says that she thinks that you would rather
live in the country. I know that where ever we buy a
house it will be right place for our future.

Kiss the kids for me.
Bob

I have been reading the books that Rebecca recommened and trying to implement the suggestions into my daily life. Keeping this journal really helps.

Working on the journal gives me something to do at night. IX It helps me deal with my grief and helps me think about all the positive things in my life and our bright future. It makes me feel like I am accomplishing something.

I am looking forward to our move to Massachusetts. I know that we will find a great house and it is a beautiful area. But there are things that I will miss about our life here. It will be hard to leave this house and all our memories. I also love that even though we are in a big city, we live on a quiet street that is more like a country lane. It is so small that it's not even on all the maps.

gold !"
' And the bird from her shelter the gust sweeps away !

'Poor Paradise Bird ! on her lone flight once more
  ' Back again in the wake of the wind she is driven—
'To be whelm'd in the storm, or above it to soar,
  ' And, if rescued from ocean, to vanish in heaven !

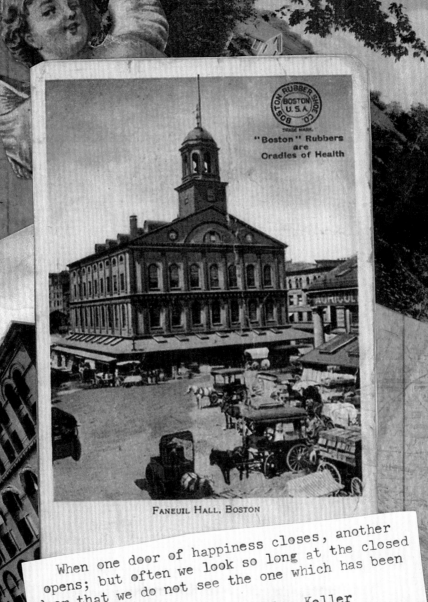

BOSTON RUBBER SHOE CO.
BOSTON
U.S.A.
TRADE MARK.

"Boston" Rubbers
are
Cradles of Health

FANEUIL HALL, BOSTON

Fishing

When one door of happiness closes, another
opens; but often we look so long at the closed
door that we do not see the one which has been
opened for us.

Helen Keller

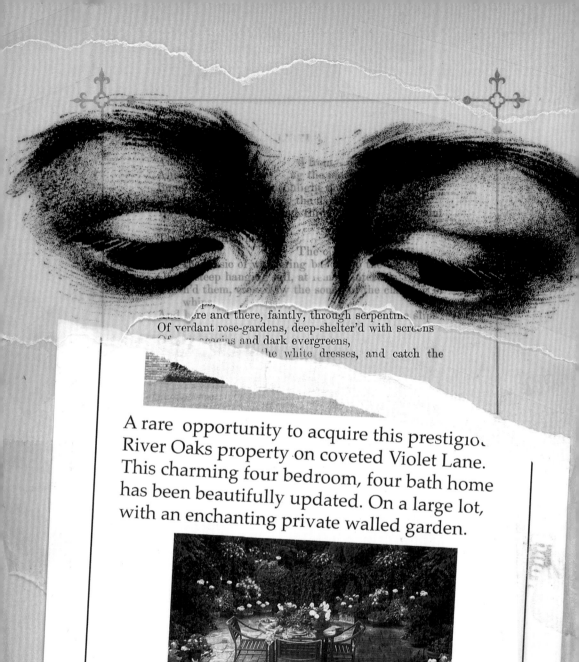

And here and there, faintly, through serpentine slips
Of verdant rose-gardens, deep-shelter'd with screens
Of acacias and dark evergreens,
the white dresses, and catch the

A rare opportunity to acquire this prestigious
River Oaks property on coveted Violet Lane.
This charming four bedroom, four bath home
has been beautifully updated. On a large lot,
with an enchanting private walled garden.

Am I being paranoid? ~~I am afraid~~ A very strange
thing happened today and I can't seem to get it
out of my mind. It's probably nothing, but it
makes me feel ~~creepy~~ uneasy.

We had to leave the house this afternoon
because it was being shown by a realtor, so
we went to the Galleria. While we were at the
Discovery Store, I looked at telescopes for
Bob's birthday next month. Susan said that she
would love it if Daddy had a telescope, because
then she could look through it. She said that
she's always wanted to look through one. I
reminded her about **Vanessa's** telescope and how
she and Alex tried to see our house from
Vanessa's condo. Susan was very emphatic about
the fact that ~~she had~~ she had never looked
through a telescope. Miss **Vanessa** said that
the telescope was very, very expensive and
they weren't ever allowed to touch it. Susan
was so definite and ~~Alex~~ Alex agreed that they
had never looked through Vanessa's telescope.

SO WHY WAS VANESSA'S TELESCOPE FOCUSED RIGHT
ON OUR HOUSE???? ~~SHE WAS SPYING ON US THE ENTIRE~~

It wasn't my imagination. ~~That took up~~ I could
see our PRIVATE patio perfectly. I felt ~~angry~~
funny at the time, but Vanessa had a ~~reaxx~~
reasonable explanation. ~~She always has an~~
~~answer for everything.~~

From: "Bob Mason" <mason2609@yahoo.com>

Subject: Telephone call

To: amyzmason@yahoo.com

Amy,

I am glad that we were able to have a long talk tonight. I was worried about how upset you were, but I hope that you are feeling better now. I've been thinking about it and I know that there are several logical explanations. It is possible that the kids were looking through the telescope and didn't want to admit it because they were told not to touch it. Or if it was Vanessa, I'm sure that she wasn't spying, but since she has that telescope, she obviously looks at things and it's only natural to try to find landmarks that you know. Maybe she was embarrassed to be caught looking at our house and said it was the kids.

I worry about how stressed out you are feeling. This time apart has been hard for me too. But we will all be together soon. I hope that you are getting enough sleep. Things can really get blown out of proportion when you are sleep deprived.

I miss you. Kiss the kids for me. I won't let anything interfere with my trip home next weekend, even though Julia would like me to stay here and attend a function with her.
Bob

The staggering light did wax and wane,
Till there came a snap of the heavy brain;
And a slow-subsiding pulse of pain;
And the whole world darkened into rest,
As the grim Earl pressed to his grausome breast
His white wife. She hung heavy there
On his shoulder without breath,

'Hush, hu...

One can learn by observing others.

Someone is watching all that you do.

What's wrong with me? Why do I have
these thoughts about Vanessa?

First I was surprised by how quickly
I felt close to her, and now I have these
suspicious/negative feelings.

Rebecca thouhgt thatit was understandable
that I felt a closeness to Vanessa. Those
sorts of attachments or friendships are common
when people are in the sort of XX situation
I've had.

Maybe I should talk to Rebecca about
my feelings of suspicion, but I am XXX
afraid to because at one of our sessions,
when I carefully mentioned feelings of
betrayal with Vanessa, I thought that
Rebeccaxx was thinking that I was XXXXXXX
jealous that Vanessa was also becoming
friends with Bob. That's wrong--I can
certainly "share" my friend.

Does not con - cern us!

The Wentworth Heart Institute

Amy,

Dr. Mason asked me to send you these real estate brochures although by the time that you get them they will be obsolete since I understand that Mrs. Wentworth prefers that you live in the city.

Thanks for the beautiful card, and it was so nice to have that long talk on the phone. We do have a lot in common, and I too feel like we're friends already. I have been looking into some art classes or workshops that we could take when you move here.

You didn't mention on the phone, but have you sold your house? I thought that something must be going on because Dr. Mason talks to Mrs. Garamond so often.

Shirley

P.S. Give me a call, we should talk.

Single Family Property, Approximately 0.38 acre(s), Lot is ... ft
built: 1856, Waterfront property, Detached home, Garage, Central air conditi...
Fireplace(s), Dining room, Laundry room, Hardwood floors

... KITCHENS, TWO STORY FOYERS. S...
... ARCHITECTURAL A...

To a...

Pre...

- ...

Ga...
He...

H...
Ho...
In...
In Le...
Lo...
Pa...

Skyli...
Ceils...
Wall...

LIVING ROOM: Woodburning fireplace wit...
dow seat,

DINING ROOM: ...

FAMILY ROOM: ...
case. Wet bar with i...

KITCHEN: Spacious...
board for coffeepot. ...
Breakfast room with b...

POWDER BATHROO...

UTILITY ROOM: Sin...

MASTER BRM: Ceiling...
Master Bath: tile floor, 2...
shower.

UPSTAIRS: accessed by ...
3 Bedrooms: all with grea...

2 Full baths.   2 Linen clos...

GAME ROOM: Can be par...
for exercise.

GARAGE: 2 car. EOHD. ...

Amy,

Thank You so much
It is so beautiful for the
of "Lalla Rookh." I had never heard
working on it.
The attachment is about the
classes we talked about the
Talk to You soon.
Shirley

new york
Linco

REBECCA
DIPL.

(713) 65
(713) 659

NAME
ADDRESS
Rx ILLEGAL IF NOT SAFETY BLU

Rx

XWWAX O.

TOTAL

REFILL ( ) TIMES

26.0

Am I being paranoid...again?
I hate to mention this to Bob because
I don't want him to think that I'm
crazy or overly dramatic.XⅪⅩⅩⅩⅩⅩⅩⅩ
XⅩⅩ And it is NOT a cry for attention!

    Did Vanessa read my journal? Is she
spying on me? When we came back to the
house today we saw only one set of footprints
in the carpet. Susan followed them and they
went into my bedroom, where they walked
around and seemed to stop at the bedside
table where I keep this Journal. Was it my
imagination or had it been moved?
    Vanessa wasstill st the house. She said
that the people never showed up. Susan
came running back downstairs and said,
"Miss Vanessa, why were you walking all
around in my mom and daddy's room?" Did
Vanessa look startled for a moment?
Vanessa said, yes she had been in my room
while she was waiting for the people. She
wentup to my room to compare some paint chips
to our wall color because "she loves my color
choices." She did pull some paint sample
charts out of her bag to show us. (to prove
that she wasn¢t snooping?)

    I don't know what to think. I am surethat
this book was moved, or am I just being
paranoid and overrecting again? She did have
those color samples. But I am still going to
move this journal. Iknow a secret place.

erature. The Belevedere summer pal... after 1916. Th... time
beautiful gardens and ponds. Near Ly... tions in this line of forecasting... splinter
Lazienski palace, built by Poniatowski, who... who are naming the republican wheels.
seated on the thr... by for... through Cat... President Wilson... ind an
...of Russia, whose favorite... he was among ...the Underwood ...by...
...r favorites. It is an im... instrument ...properly tested un...
...Jur... t reposing lions, commemorating Polish... not been in effect a...
...erals, who were killed fighting for th... upset every calculation... Paris
...in the Polish upri... upon all lines of Ame...
...part of the city... oneously charged to... ts into
...structed in imitati... a grave question whi... with a
Paris. ...listen to campaign... f solid
This is a glim... ...faces
af... hundred... ...to dis... coun-
fi... e in the greatest war of all. ...for the... planets

Sullivan, the Man, ...be intere...

(From the Owensboro Messe... the Und... ew low
Roger Sullivan made th... ...ff discuss... to: pre-
democrat ever ran... outrage knew... place
State of I... at the outset of th...
vote ...ugh the Canadian re... terri-
mer... two years that the... obacco
legislat... two years... ...b of revising the ta... ighest-
James... (democrat) was elected ...sked that a halt be...
...ng with the tariff...
...calculations m...
...ttempt is made to p...
...n that issue. Esp...
...he war subsides in ti...
...ed business uplift...

...cotton situation
...g and currency
...ccasion little surpr...
...well enough alon...
...o a tedious tariff
...republicans will hav...
...k for the creation...
...rious schedules a...
...g. If they shoul...
...gress and elect...
...pt to m...
...mary...
...by
...which...
...tisfy the...
...ned by a...
...forward...

hear is a poem for
you 1, 2 I ♥ you
you ♥ me to.
wright back PS

his says Hi

Life leaves us so.
Love dare not stay.
Sweet things decay.

    I hate for Susan and Alex to see me like
this. I am trying to fight it ~~but it seems~~
~~hopeless~~. I know that things will be better for
them soon.

Dear Bob,

I feel so much better. You don't have to worry about me. I know I sounded like a mess on the phone last night. But I've had such a great day. I feel so relaxed.

Vanessa can be very thoughtful. She called to say that two agents wanted to show the house today, and I had to be gone from 10 to 2. Just when I was thinking "what am I going to do for 4 hours?" she said that she had a surprise for me and she'd come get me.

I was so surprised—she took me to the Spa at the Houston Hotel and we had a sauna and massage. Since I have never had a spa massage, I was a little embarrassed, but it was wonderful. Now I see why Vanessa loves that place. The massage was so relaxing and the place has such a soothing atmosphere. The only trouble was that the time went too fast. I didn't want to leave.

I am so glad that you will be here most of next week. Since Mrs. Wentworth is coming to Houston to see some of the programs at the Medical Center, will you have to spend all your time with her? Do we really have to go to that fundraiser with her on Saturday night?

Call us tonight if you get a chance.
Love,
Amy

The whole case, believe me, is totally changed,
And a letter may alter the plans we arranged
Over-night, for the slaughter of Time—a wild beast,

Amy,

Bob has already been invaluable to us, but I know it has been at the expense of his not being home.

I heard how much you enjoyed your day at the Spa. This is my thank you for all you are doing to make it possible for Bob to be here.

Julia

Your Gift

The flattering fires of life grow dim
About my heart. And off in
Lying whole hours awake

Houston Spa and Resort

Houston Spa and Resort

pure bliss . . .

Menu of Services

Let me think . . . my head is aching.
I have little strength to think.
And I know my heart is breaking.

I can't believe that Mrs. Wentworth gave me
this gift! It is such a surprise. The timing is
perfect, since Bob will be home for some stuff
at the Medical Center. The children are so
excited about spending time with Daddy that they
won;t even miss me. Bob is such a good dad
and he will be able to handle it when I'm not
there.

I never thought about doing anything like this.
It seems so self-indulgent. I know that I will
finally get the rest I need. It is such a
peaceful place.

Fear? . . . I cannot fear! for fear
    Dies with hope in every breast.
O, I see the frozen sneer,
    Careless smile, and callous jest!

But my shame shall yet be worn
    Like the purple of a queen.
I can answer scorn with scorn.
    Fool! I know not what I mean.

Yet beneath his smile (*his* smile!)
    Smiles less kind I shall not see.
Let the whole wide world revile.
    He is all the world to me.

So to-night all hopes, all fears,
    All the bright and brief array
Of my lost youth's happier years,
    With these gems I put away.

Gone! . . . so . . . one by one . . . all gone!
    Not one jewel I retain
Of my life's wealth. All alone
    I tread boldly o'er my pain

On to him . . . Ah, me! my child—
    My own fair-haired, darling boy!
In his sleep just now he smiled.
    All his dreams are dreams of joy.

How those soft long lashes shade
    That young cheek so husht and warm,
Like a half-blown rosebud laid
    On the little dimpled arm!

He will wake without a mother.
    He will hate me when he hears
From the cold lips of another
    All my faults in after years.

Amy's journal ended here. We were curious about her, so we did an internet search to see if we could find out anything about her. Here are the articles that we found in the Houston newspaper archives.

K. A. and J. A.

Than as youth loves, when our wild
     New-found passions master us.

And——for I was proud of old
     ('T is my nature)——doubtless she
In the man so calm, so cold,
     All the heart's warmth could not see.

Nay, I blame myself——nor lightly,
     Whose chief duty was to guide
Her young careless life more rightly
     Through the perils at her side.

Ah, but love is blind! and I
     Loved her blindly, blindly! . . . Well,
Who that ere loved trustfully
     Such strange danger could fortell?

As some consecrated cup
     On its saintly shrine secure,
All my life seemed lifted up
     On that heart I deemed so pure.

Well, for me there yet remains
     Labor——that 's much: then, the state:
And what pays a thousand pains,
     Sense of right and scorn of fate.

THE WIFE'S TRAGEDY.

And about her the armorial
   Scutcheons of a haughty race,
Graven each with its memorial
   Of the old Lords of the Place.

You, who do profess to see
   In the face the written mind,
Look in that face, and tell me
   In what part of it you find

All the falsehood, and the wrong,
   And the sin, which must have been
Hid in baleful beauty long,
   Like the worm that lurks unseen

In the shut heart of the flower.
   'T is the sex, no doubt!   And still
Some may lack the means, the power,
   There 's not one that lacks the will.

Their own way they seek the Devil,
   Ever prone to the deceiver!
If too deep I feel this evil
   And this shame, may God forgive her!

For I loved her,—loved, ay, loved her
   As a man just once may love.
I so trusted, so approved her,
   Set her, blindly, so above

This poor world which was about her,
   And (so loving her) because,
With a faith too high to doubt her,
   I, forsooth, but seldom was

At her feet with clamorous praises
   And protested tenderness
(These things some men can do), phrases
   On her face, perhaps her dress,

✉ Email This Story   🖶 Print This Story

Local Woman Found Dead in Downtown Hotel

HOUSTON--Employees of a downtown hotel discovered the body of a local woman Sunday morning. The woman, identified as Amy Zoe Mason, 34, of River Oaks, was a guest at the Houston Hotel and Spa. Police have not yet determined the cause of death. Lily Gomez, a maid at the hotel, reported finding an empty bottle of prescription pills in Mrs. Mason's room

Mrs. Mason had checked into the hotel Saturday afternoon to take advantage of the hotel's spa services. Julia Wentworth, speaking for the family, said that Mrs. Mason's visit to the spa was a gift. Mrs. Mason, mother of two, had been under a great deal of stress due to the recent death of her mother and an imminent move to Boston, where her husband, Dr. Robert Mason, relocated in January. "I know that Amy had trouble sleeping," said Wentworth, "but she was looking forward to the family's move to Massachusetts."

Family friend, Vanessa Garamond, said, "I know that her overdose had to be an accident. This is a terrible loss to her family. I have lost a great friend."

According to attendants at the Houston Spa, Mrs. Mason enjoyed her spa treatments Saturday afternoon. Emma Johnson, massage therapist, reported that Mrs. Mason said that she hadn't felt so good in months and that the spa visit was just what she needed. Hotel employee, Tony D'Onofrio, reported that Mrs. Mason seemed surprised and happy with a gift of flowers and champagne that he delivered to her room at 7:30 pm on Saturday evening. "She seemed like a nice lady," said D'Onofrio. "She said that she was really having a relaxing stay."

Craig Patterson, manager of the Houston Hotel and Spa, said, "We are deeply saddened by this event. The hotel and staff extend our condolences to Mrs. Mason's family."

In (

Susp
Robl
Astro
High

See (
Secti(

Which he gave me long ago.
  'T was upon my bridal eve,
When I swore to love him so
  As a wife should—smile or grieve

With him, for him,—and not shrink.
  And now? . . . O the long, long pain !
See this sunken cheek ! You think
  He would know my face again ?

All its wretched beauty gone !
  Only the deep care survives.
Ah, could years of grief atone
  For those fatal hours ! . . . It drives

Past the pane, the bitter blast !
  In this garret one might freeze.
Hark there ! wheels below ! At last
  He is come then ? No . . . the trees

And the night-wind—nothing more !
  Set the chair for him to sit,
When he comes. And close the door,
  For the gust blows cold through it.

When I think, I can remember
  I was born in castle halls,—
How yon dull and dying ember
  Glares against the whitewasht walls !

If he come not (but you said
  That the messenger was sent
Long since ?) Tell him when I'm dead
  How my life's last hours were spent

In repenting that life's sin,
  And . . . the room grows strangely dark !
See, the rain is oozing in.
  Set the lamp down nearer. Hark,

Footsteps, footsteps on the stairs!
   His . . . no, no! 't was *not* the wind.
God, I know, has heard my prayers.
   We shall meet.   I am resigned.

Prop me up upon the pillows.
   Will he come to my bedside?
Once 't was his . . . Among the willows
   How the water seems to glide!

Past t   forms the towers,
   It s
" Dea
   I h

" He
  On
Ah, i
  A

Say

Ge

B
W

G

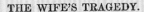

NEWS   **SPORTS**   **ENTERTAINMEN**

AMY ZOE MASON

View/Sign Guestboo

AMY ZOE MASON, 34, beloved mother, wife, daughter
and friend, passed away in Houston, Texas on Saturday.
Amy was born in Ames, Iowa to Patrick and Mary Brown.
She is preceded in death by both parents. Amy moved to
Houston three years ago with her husband and children.
She is survived by her loving husband, Dr. Robert Mason
and her two children, Susan and Alexander, who were the
center of her life. Amy was a gifted artist, devoted friend
and active volunteer at River Oaks Elementary School.
She found great joy and fulfillment in her role as mother
and wife. A private service for family members will be
held Saturday, at 4:00 pm. In lieu of flowers, memorial
donations may be sent to The Wentworth Heart Institute,
Boston, Massachusetts.

GERTRUDE.

               Will you stand
   Near me?   Sit down.   Do not stir.
Tell me, may I take your hand?
   Tell me, will you look on her

Grant–Garamond Realty

Vanessa Garamond, President

Grant–Garamond Realty is Houston's Premiere Real Estate Company, specializing in fine properties for over 40 years.

Dear Friends,

After serving the River Oaks area for over 40 years, Grant–Garamond Realty is closing its office. I am sad to be leaving my friends and colleagues, but I am looking forward to the next chapter in my life. I have married a wonderful man and become the mother to his two delightful children. We now live in Boston, where my husband, Dr. Robert Mason, is the Director of the Wentworth Heart Institute.

Thank you for the kind wishes. It has been a pleasure working with each and every one of you.

Vanessa Garamond Mason

After we saw Vanessa's business website, Grant-Garamond.com, we wanted to find out more about Vanessa and Bob. Our sister lives in Manchester, New Hampshire, and reads the Boston papers. We asked her to send us anything that she came across that mentioned Bob or Vanessa. She sent us these articles.

K. A. and J. A.

O, when all seemed g————
    I was weak—I cannot tell—
But the serpent in my ear
    Whispered, whispered—and I fell.

Look around, now.   Does it cheer you,
    This strange place? the wasted frame
Of the dying woman near you,
    Weighed into her grave by shame?

Can you trace in this wan form
    Aught resembling that young girl's
Whom you loved once?   See, this arm—
    Shrunken, shrunken!   And my curls,

They have cut them all away.
    And my brows are worn with woe,
Would you, looking at me, say,
    She was lovely long ago?

Husband, answer! in all these
    Are you not avenged?   If I
Could rise now, upon my knees,
    At your feet, before I die,

I would fall down in my sorrow
    And my shame, and say "forgive,"
That which will be dust to-morrow,
    This weak clay!
    15*

This is from a Boston daily newspaper website.

Home & Garden   Weddings   Fashion   Health & Fitness   Entertainment

Weddings

ANNOUNCEMENT   WEDDING DETAILS   PHOTO GALLERY   GUEST BOOK

WEDDING ANNOUNCEMENT
Vanessa Garamond & Robert Mason

Vanessa Garamond and Dr. Robert Mason were married at the beautiful country home of close friend, Julia Wentworth. The groom's children, Susan and Alexander, acted as the attendants. The reception was held on the riverfront grounds of Mrs. Wentworth's estate. Following a honeymoon in Switzerland, the Masons will reside in Boston.

Send to a friend   Printer-friendly format

Planning your wedding? Browse these area vendors

Bridal Shops   Caterers   Flowers and Decor   Reception Sites   Invitations   Photography

Did he ever ask to see?
Has he grown to love another—
Some strange woman not like me?

Opera Guild Co-Chairs, Dr. Patrick Ryan and Vanessa Mason

Opera Guild Sparkles

Tony party-goers danced the night away last Saturday evening at the Opera Guild Ball. The event was co-chaired by **Dr. Patrick Ryan** and Boston's favorite newcomer, the glamorous **Vanessa Mason**. Mrs. Mason brought some of her Texas sparkle to the gala. Joining in the fun were **Mrs. Diane Ryan, Dr. Robert Mason, Dr. and Mrs. Daniel Edwards, Chip** and **Suzy Williams, Julia Wentworth, Preston** and **Mia Parkinson, Theodore Blakely III** and his lovely ~~Georgia Stewart~~, **Gloria Monroe** and her

Vanessa Mason and Dr. Daniel Edwards attend the first annual Jonathan Wentworth Memorial Philanthropic Award Luncheon.

The L
Wome
garder

or the
harity
by all.

Smith-James contributed touch to the fashion scene.

Mother-Daughter Festivities

It was sugar and spice, and all things nice as mothers and daughters gathered for the Annual Mother-Daughter Holiday Tea fundraiser held in the exquisite Oval Room of the Copley Plaza Hotel. Amid stunning seasonal decorations, mothers and daughters were treated to a sumptuous English Tea of tea sandwiches, scones and Devonshire cream, an assortment of mini-pastries and of course, the Copley's beautiful Tuile Basket with White Mousse and Berries. The festive holiday event, which benefits Boston area children in need, was chaired by the dynamic duo of **Margaret (Muffy) Adams** and daughter **Beatrice (Buffy)**. Charming **Elizabeth Morgan** and daughter, **Paige Frances** co-chaired the event, with assistance from auburn-haired newcomers, **Vanessa Mason** and her lovely daughter, **Susan**. Among those in attendance were, **Mary** and **Rebecca Foster-Schieffer**, **Nancy** and **Louisa Fenton**, **Shelley** and **Amanda Blane**, **Georgia** and **Carolyn Houghton**, and **Helen O'Brien** and her daughter **Nicole Evans**. Guests were delighted by the holiday entertainment provided by the St. Patrick's Children's Choir, followed by the lilting sounds of harpist Jennifer Soames-Ashe.

Just Friends

Was Cupid aiming his arrow at the stunning Joanna Simons-Hughes on Saturday night at
the Wilt…

CANTO

'But
'Tha

'Free

He re
'He
a
'Dare
'Whi
'I ma
'Wha
'Free

She s

As he
All tl
And
Of wi
And
From
In th
Hum
As th
And
By al
To in
And o

What
n
The
'
Can

That

FASHION
Stevenson
reign supre…

People Who Make a Difference

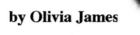

A Love That Never Dies

by Olivia James

It is hard to imagine a more devoted couple than Jonathan and Julia Wentworth, and that devotion continues, although Jonathan Wentworth died ten years ago. Since her husband's death, Mrs. Wentworth has worked tirelessly to establish The Jonathan Wentworth Heart Institute in his honor. "Working towards this goal, I often felt Jonathan's presence at my side," said the still lovely Mrs. Wentworth.

Jonathan Wentworth was a widower when he met the beautiful debutante, Julia Smith Hargrave, fifty years ago. After a whirlwind romance, Jonathan and Julia surprised everyone by becoming one of Boston's most devoted couples. They spent their time together co-chairing highly successful fundraising activities for a variety of charitable organizations. "Jonathan was the most wonderful man. The age difference never bothered us," recalled Mrs. Wentworth. "In fact, he was at the point in his life where he was able to devote most of his energies to his humanitarian interests. I shared his vision." Both Mr. and Mrs. Wentworth came from families with a long tradition of philanthropy.

"After Jonathan's death from heart disease, I decided to establish The Jonathan Wentworth Heart Institute in his honor. Although we never had children, the legacy of this wonderful man will continue with the institute that carries his name," said Mrs. Wentworth.

The mission of The Wentworth Heart Institute is to serve humanity through innovative cardiovascular research, public and physician education and improved patient care, focusing on prevention, early detection and treatment. "Our cardiac research will help people to live longer, with a better quality of life. New technologies and our excellent staff are already putting us on the map," says Mrs. Wentworth proudly.

Leading that staff is Dr. Robert Mason, whom Mrs. Wentworth lured away from the Texas Medical Center in Houston. "Choosing Robert Mason was one of my best decisions," said Mrs. Wentworth. "Although everyone on the board was impressed with his pioneering work, some thought that he was too young to be director. However, I could see in Dr. Mason the drive necessary to help create my vision. I am happy to say that the board now enthusiastically gives Dr. Mason their full support."

Community outreach and education are also important goals of the Institute. Already a highly successful fundraising organization is in place for this purpose, responsible for some of Boston's most highly anticipated events, including the Institute's Spring Gala. Spearheading the fundraising events is Vanessa Mason, wife of Dr. Robert Mason. Mrs. Mason was a successful businesswoman in Houston, with a history of chairing high-profile fundraising events. When she married Dr. Mason she brought her expertise to Boston. "It was a auspicious day when Vanessa joined the Wentworth family," said Mrs. Wentworth. "She has brought fresh ideas, and the vitality of the Masons has attracted a younger set of donors. An unexpected personal benefit has been the close friendship that I have developed with the Masons. They have become my family."

"I look back on the last ten years and know that I did what was necessary to make the Institute a success no matter what the personal sacrifice. The Institute has become more important than any one person."

PHOTO: OWEN ROLF

STRIKING COUPLE: Dr. Robert Mason and his lovely wife, Vanessa, were co-chairs of the Third Annual Spring Gala benefiting the Wentworth Heart Institute.

Spectacular Gala
Third Time is a Charm

The third annual Spring Gala, to benefit The Wentworth Heart Institute community outreach and education programs, was a resounding success as Boston's beautiful people danced the night away at the Ritz-Carlton on Saturday evening. The event was co-chaired by Dr. Robert Mason, Director of The Wentworth Heart Institute and his vivacious wife, Vanessa Mason. Partygoers were stunned by the spectacular decor which transformed the ballroom into a spring garden. Floral design by Boston